CW01090628

ALEX DARKFELL

# Midnight and Other Short Stories

To Lauren

Hope you enjoy!

Best wishes

AD

Seaglass Press

First edition

ISBN (paperback): 978-1-0683332-1-7
ISBN (hardcover): 978-1-0683332-2-4

This book was professionally typeset on Reedsy.
Find out more at reedsy.com

# Contents

# Acknowledgments

First and foremost, I would like to express my deepest gratitude to my wife, **Emma,** and our two wonderful boys, **Kilian** and **Dax**, for their unwavering love, patience and understanding during the writing of this book. Your support and encouragement have been invaluable in helping me to balance the demands of work, family life and my passion for writing.

I am also incredibly grateful to my editor, **Francesca Tyer,** for her exceptional insights, meticulous attention to detail and insightful suggestions. Your expertise has been instrumental in shaping this book into its final form.

# 1

# The Time Between

***Author's Note***

*'The Time Between' has had a few different iterations before emerging into the world as the story you're about to read. As the longest story in this collection, it was one that I rewrote several times to try to ensure I grasped the tone right . It came from a consideration of loss and grief and the thought that if you were given the choice to live in a dream which you could make into what you wanted, knowing it wasn't real, or to keep living your current life, working through the sorrow and loss, which would you choose? To be clear, I don't believe there is a correct answer to this in any absolute sense. The 'correctness' of the decision should be personal to the individual, as is the processing of grief itself. If this is something you, dear reader, are going through right now, know that we're never really alone in this world, despite what it may feel.*

*Warnings: Loss, Grief*

The letter arrived on a Tuesday, exactly six months after Ash's funeral. Xanthe had just returned from another relentless night shift at the hospital, and despite ditching her scrubs and showering before she left, she still reeked of antiseptic. Her hands red raw from the constant application of hand sanitizer. She almost missed the envelope beneath the usual pile of bills and junk mail, her sleep deprived mind not wanting to register anything apart from the prospect of her bed.

It was the lettering that first caught her eye. Her name, Xanthe Lowell, and her address all written in elegant, golden calligraphy. The letters shimmered, despite the dim morning light seeping through the hallway window. The paper was thick, like parchment, and warm to the touch. There was no postage stamp or post mark, but the back was adorned with a large, blue wax seal.

Dropping the rest of the junk mail back on the doormat, Xanthe carefully broke the seal and unfolded the letter, revealing more of the elegant golden script. It was an invitation but unlike any she'd seen before.

*To the esteemed Xanthe Lowell,*
*On this night when the veil grows thin,*
*Where grief will cease and dreams begin,*
*Your presence is humbly requested*
*At The Time Between, where pain is bested.*

*A grand ball, where memories dance,*
*We offer you a singular chance*
*To step beyond the bounds of day,*
*And let your cares all fall away.*

2

*What was lost may yet be found,*
  *In this place where time's unbound.*
  *One night of wonder, free from sorrow,*
  *A respite from the hollow tomorrow.*

*R.S.V.P. unnecessary – your heart will guide you.*
  *Yours in eternal anticipation,*
  *The Timeless Host*

Xanthe read through the words three times, her sleep deprived mind not quite accepting what she was holding. Was this a joke? She glanced at the urn on the mantelpiece, sitting next to her favorite photo from a trip to France from two summers back. It was a lifetime ago, from a time when the future seemed limitless. Ash's arm was around her waist and their smiles reflected their happiness. She could recall the moment perfectly. The sun on their faces, the warmth of Ash's body against hers, the feeling that this was forever.

But forever had ended.

For the past six months, time had caught in a loop. She had always loved seeing her friends but they'd all become strangers now. She couldn't face the same questions, the same sympathetic looks as if she were made of glass and that even a loud noise would shatter her.

Xanthe looked back down at the invitation and sighed. "I need some sleep," she murmured.

Exhaustion weighed on every step as she climbed the stairs alone to her bedroom. She placed the invitation on her nightstand and wearily undressed. As she slipped underneath the cool sheets, her mind drifted to Ash. She pushed the thoughts away as she closed her eyes.

*"What was lost may yet be found*
  *In this place where time's unbound."*

She tried to empty her thoughts, but the memory of the golden script kept surfacing in her mind, pushing sleep aside.

*"One night of wonder, free from sorrow,*
  *A respite from the hollow tomorrow."*

Realizing sleep wasn't going to come, she sat up, trying to rub the weariness from her eyes. The invitation sat there next to her, the early morning sunshine reflecting off the golden ink.

Xanthe reached for it and read it again. There was nothing on it to say where or when the supposed ball was to take place or even how she should respond.

*"R.S.V.P. unnecessary – your heart will guide you."*

What did that even mean? She glanced at the clock. It was barely 7 AM, and her next shift wasn't until the following night. The day stretched before her, empty and hollow like all the others these past six months.

"I can't keep living like this," she whispered to the empty room. "Ash wouldn't want me to."

Dropping the invitation back on the bed, she moved to her closet, pushing aside the sea of practical wear that had become her uniform both on and off duty. In the back, hidden away like a relic from another life, hung the dress she'd worn on her last anniversary with Ash. It was a deep midnight blue, scattered with tiny sequins that sparkled like stars. Ash had said she looked like the night sky come to life.

4

She slipped it on. It was the first time she'd worn it for over a year and despite it feeling a little loose on her now, she was pleased to see that it still fitted reasonably well. She stepped toward, facing her large mirror, examining the figure which stood before her. She ran her hands down her body, feeling the smooth fabric as it hugged her, trying to suppress the thought of Ash and the memory of the night she last wore it. She hadn't really looked at herself for so long, she could see new lines around her eyes, lines made by something that went much deeper than the lack of sleep.

She wanted to feel the way she used to, when life felt simpler and fuller. She wanted to see the old Xanthe looking back at her. She found a pair of heels hidden in a box on top of her closet and slipped them on. She took her hairbrush from her nightstand and pulled it through the thick knots of her light brown hair. The old Xanthe was in there somewhere, she just needed some help to come out.

Standing in front of the mirror, she finally saw her. The old Xanthe stood taller; her shoulders not yet hunched with grief. A spark of life was visible in her eyes, a hint of the woman she used to be. The old Xanthe took a deep breath, feeling the fabric of the dress expand with her chest, and for the first time in what felt like forever, she allowed herself a small smile.

Xanthe walked back over to the bed and picked up the invitation, running her fingers over its golden lettering, and in as loud a voice as she could manage, she said, "I accept."

The paper dissolved in her hands, its golden particles swirling as the room began to blur until her vision consisted only of her own reflection surrounded by a sea of gold. The world spun, a dizzying kaleidoscope of gold and blue. Xanthe closed her eyes, feeling weightless but grounded at the same time. When the spinning stopped, she opened them slowly, blinking to take in her new surroundings.

She was standing in a doorway leading to an enormous ballroom. Its ceiling was so high that she couldn't make out where the walls ended, and the stars began. Chandeliers hung low all around, their crystals shining, casting a soft glow throughout the room. Grand, orchestral music filled the space, seemingly coming from everywhere.

As her eyes adjusted to the soft, golden light, Xanthe began to make out people around the room. Some in the center of the room were dancing together, their forms flickering. They swirled around, some dressed in elaborate gowns and suits, seemingly from centuries past, while others sparkled in clothes Xanthe couldn't comprehend.

She took a few, tentative steps into the room, her heels clicking on the polished marble floor. Around the edges, she saw more people, mostly standing alone watching the dancers as they spun to the music. Xanthe's eyes widened as she took in their appearances. It was like they'd all been displaced, staring around in disbelief, the walls around them shimmering like water.

"Welcome, Xanthe Lowell," a voice suddenly whispered in her ear, the sound occupying her whole mind at once. She spun on the spot but there was no-one nearby.

"Who... who are you? Wh... what is this place?" she managed to stutter.

"I am your host," the voice said again as Xanthe recoiled. "Do not be afraid, you are my guest at The Time Between, where past, present and future intertwine. Here time has no meaning, and the boundaries between what was, what is and what could be, blur together."

6

Xanthe's head spun. No-one else seemed to have heard the voice.

"We will meet soon," it continued, smooth like honey. "For now, please enjoy the spectacle."

Xanthe tried to calm herself and process what was happening. The voice faded, leaving her alone amidst the swirling dancers and shimmering walls.

She looked around the room again, trying to center herself on something. Making her way to the nearest wall she noticed a young man, perhaps in his early twenties. He was dressed in a dark, three-piece suit, the light from the chandeliers reflecting from the glass-like shine of his formal black shoes.

Without hesitation, Xanthe took a few steps toward him. His gaze flickered to her, and she saw fear flash in his eyes before he darted his gaze back to the dancers. She could almost feel his internal struggle as he debated whether to stay or make a hasty escape.

Xanthe moved quickly before he could make up his mind. At the hospital, she'd had a lot of experience talking to people who didn't want to open up and she realized she'd have to use all of her carefully cultivated bedside manner if she wanted to find out anything from this man.

"Hello," she offered carefully. His eyes flickered back up at her as she stood before him. "My name is Xanthe; may I ask yours?"

The young man hesitated, his eyes darting around the room before settling back on Xanthe. He swallowed hard.

"William," he said quietly. "William Hart."

Xanthe smiled encouragingly. "It's nice to meet you, William. Are you as confused by all of this as I am?"

William nodded and Xanthe was relieved to see his shoulders

relax slightly.

"I... I don't understand any of it", he stuttered. "I've never seen anything like this. The people, the way some of them look. How is this even possible?"

"Do you know how you got here?" Xanthe asked.

"I received an invitation," William said, his eyes finally meeting hers. "How I got here, I don't know."

They stood in silence for a moment as they took in each other's appearances. William's hair was smart and slicked back and Xanthe noticed a small golden pocket watch chain looping out from his waistcoat pocket. She had only seen people dressed like this in old pictures.

"This might sound like a strange question," Xanthe started, not quite believing what she was about to ask, "but what year is it to you?"

William furrowed his brow, and Xanthe saw the fear and distrust return to his eyes. Worried she'd spooked him, she tried to reassure him with a smile.

"I know! It sounds so silly doesn't it?" she said, trying to sound relaxed. "But if you wouldn't mind humoring me? It's OK, you can trust me. I'm just trying to find out what's going on here." She placed a reassuring hand on his shoulder.

William gave a tentative smile and glanced nervously at her hand.

"1916," he finally said.

Xanthe's breath caught in her throat. 1916? She tried to keep her expression neutral, not wanting to alarm William further.

"Thank you," she said softly. "And... are you here alone?"

William's eyes clouded. "Yes, I don't have any family, you see. My father and both of my brothers died recently, in the war. It's just me now."

8

Xanthe looked at him sadly. He was just a boy, the fear in his eyes now making sense to her.

"The invitation," he continued, whispering over the swelling music "it said I could see them again. Just for one night."

Xanthe's heart ached for him. She understood that desperate hope, the longing to see a loved one just one more time.

"Have you seen them?" she asked gently.

William shook his head, his eyes glistening. "Not yet. I've been too afraid to move. What if... what if they're not here?"

Xanthe squeezed his shoulder reassuringly. "There's only one way to find out. Would you like me to help you look?"

After a brief, hesitant look, William nodded. Xanthe offered him her arm, and he took it gratefully. Together, they began to make their way around the edges of the ballroom, peering at the faces of the other guests.

As the pair made their way through the crowd, the young man's grip on her arm tightened. The ballroom seemed to stretch endlessly, its boundaries blurring into a starry void.

Xanthe's eyes were drawn to a woman standing alone, her clothing a strange mix of styles that she couldn't quite place. Their eyes met, and something passed between them, but then the woman's gaze lowered, disappointment etched on her face.

Gently, Xanthe led William over toward her.

"Hello," Xanthe said as they approached. "I'm Xanthe, and this is William. Are you... are you looking for someone too?"

The woman nodded, her eyes flickering uncertainly between them both.

"I'm Amara. I'm looking for my wife, Zara. I'd... hoped she'd be here. What year are you both from?"

The directness of the question struck Xanthe and she glanced nervously at William, worried how he'd react.

Amara's lips turned in a sad smile. "I'm from 2089, or I was. I'm not sure time means anything here."

William's grip on Xanthe's arm tightened again, his eyes wide with disbelief.

"Have you seen her? Your wife?" Xanthe asked, pushing aside her shock to focus on Amara's pain.

Amara shook her head. "Not yet," she said softly, "but I'll keep looking. I have to believe she's here somewhere. It's what the invite said, right?"

Xanthe nodded, understanding the desperate hope in Amara's eyes. So they'd all received the same invitation.

"May I ask, did something happen to Zara? In your time, I mean."

Amara stayed silent for a while, her eyes drifting over to the swirling dancers, trying to hide the tears that had started to well.

"Yes. There was a fault in her neural link. I'd warned her the tech was too new but she wouldn't have any of it. I lost her."

"I'm so sorry," Xanthe said, reaching out to gently touch Amara's arm.

Amara nodded and offered Xanthe a small smile. "Thank you. Whatever you're both here for, I hope it's worth it."

As Amara moved away, melting into the crowd, Xanthe turned to William. His face was pale, his eyes wide with confusion and fear.

"Are you alright?" Xanthe asked gently.

William shook his head slowly. "I don't understand any of this. The future... it sounds like something out of H.G. Wells."

Xanthe couldn't help but chuckle and she squeezed his hand gently, allowing herself to relax slightly when William returned her smile.

"Come on, let's keep looking," she told him.

As they continued their round of the room, Xanthe noticed the music getting louder and faster. The movements of the dancers at the center of the room were growing quicker, more intricate and the expressions on their faces never changed from the wide smiles which didn't quite reach their eyes.

William kept scanning the faces of everyone they passed as he searched for his family. Xanthe kept her gaze fixed as best she could on the dancers. If this really was a place outside of time and reality, could he be here? Would she turn around and see Ash staring back at her? She couldn't allow herself to think it, there had been too much pain; she had worked too hard to be caught by false hope now.

The tempo of the music kept increasing, the dancers moving faster and faster in perfect timing. Xanthe saw with increasing alarm that while their smiles never faltered, their eyes were wild as if caught in panic. She could see the worry growing in the faces of the other guests too as they watched, transfixed, as the dancers moved in a way she'd never seen before.

The music reached a crescendo, the dancers spinning faster than ever, their forms now just a blur of color. Xanthe wanted to stop it all, to help them, but before she could act, the music mercifully slowed, the dancers coming to a complete stop in time with the music as if they were marionettes at the end of a display.

Silence fell across the whole room. No one dared move; the only sound Xanthe could hear was the pounding of her own heart.

One-by-one, the dancers moved into a circle, facing outwards toward the guests. Xanthe watched uneasily as they robotically bowed in perfect unison, their desperate eyes betraying their fixed, permanent smiles.

"Welcome, my dear guests," a voice boomed over them. "I am your Host, and I am so pleased to see you all."

Xanthe spun wildly around, searching for the source of the voice.

"I hope you enjoyed dancing," the voice said, echoing from all directions. "After all, we're all here for some... diversion."

On that final word, everyone spun toward the ring of dancers. In unison, the dancers turned and marched away, leaving a lone figure standing in the center of the room.

The figure was tall and moved gracefully but it was difficult to make out any details. It was dressed in a suit that seemed to shift between styles with each movement. Its face was handsome but unsettling, never quite resolving into a fixed appearance. It was like trying to focus on a dream.

"My guests of honor," the figure continued. "I am your host for the evening. You have all been invited here from across time to this special occasion." The Host gestured grandly around the room as it continued to step toward. "Here, we may seek respite from our everyday torment. For it is here we make our reality what we want. If only for one night." The Host gazed around, arms outstretched as if embracing them all, its eyes constantly shifting colors like an oil slick on water. "Now is the moment, my friends..." the Host stated grandly, its ever-shifting face seeming to focus on each guest individually at the same time. "The moment for you to have what you seek."

Xanthe felt a ripple pass through all the guests as Williams grip on her arm began to loosen. She saw his eyes, now wide with longing. She looked back to where the Host was standing and with a final streak of a smile, it flickered and vanished.

The ballroom immediately erupted into chaos. People began calling out names, pushing through the crowd, their eyes wild with desperation and hope. Xanthe felt William let go of her arm as he stepped away, his gaze darting around the room.

"William," Xanthe breathed, reaching for him, but he was already gone, lost in the crowd.

"I have to find them!" he shouted.

"William, wait!" Xanthe called after him, but it was too late. All around, people were pushing past each other as they searched for their loved ones. She saw Amara calling frantically before she too was lost to the crowd.

The chaos around was overwhelming – people crying out names, the walls of the huge ballroom shimmering and rippling. Xanthe felt her breath quicken, threatening to plunge her into panic. She closed her eyes. She couldn't give in, she had to resist, something was wrong about all of this.

But something was pushing back. No matter how hard she fought, she couldn't resist the pull, until the word, barely audible, finally left her lips.

"Ash."

Silence. The noise and chaos of the room was gone, replaced by the feeling of sunshine and a cool breeze on her face. Slowly, Xanthe opened her eyes.

She was standing on a wooden veranda. Behind her, a pair of sliding doors lead inside a wooden cabin. All around, there were similar cabins, dotted along a mountainside, clear blue sky and warm sun surrounding them all. It was idyllic and she knew exactly where she was. She was in southern France, and this was her honeymoon.

"Xanthe."

She hadn't heard that voice for over six months.

"Xanthe, come on, come back to bed."

Taking a deep breath, Xanthe slowly turned. There he was,

looking exactly like he had back then. His dark hair was slightly tousled by the breeze, his green eyes sparkling with life and love.

"Ash?" Xanthe whispered, her voice trembling. She wanted to run to him, to throw her arms around him, but she held herself back.

Ash smiled softly. "It's okay. I know this is strange, but it's me. For tonight, at least."

Xanthe took a tentative step toward, then another, until she was standing right before him. "How is this possible?" she asked, her hand reaching out to touch Ash's cheek.

Ash leaned into her touch, his eyes closing briefly. "I'm not entirely sure. But I'm here. We're here, together, just like before."

Xanthe's hand trembled against his cheek, the warmth of his skin exactly as she remembered. Her resolve began to crumble as he turned his face to kiss her palm, just like he used to do.

"I've missed you so much," she whispered, her voice breaking.

"I know."

Ash pulled her closer, and Xanthe found herself melting into him. His familiar scent, the way his arms fitted perfectly around her – it was overwhelming. When his lips found hers, she knew she should resist, but instead, surrendered to it.

Time seemed to stop as they held each other. Xanthe could feel tears on her cheeks but didn't know if they were hers or his. For just a moment, she allowed herself to forget everything else – the funeral, the lonely nights, the grief that had become her constant companion. The familiar warmth of his body against hers melting away the loneliness and grief of the past six months. She felt his hands on her back, reigniting sensations she'd thought she'd never feel again. She pulled her fingers through his hair, letting the memories of their life together wash over her.

She felt his strong arms guiding her and while she knew it couldn't be real, she let him take control.

"Wait," Xanthe said catching his hand gently.

Ash paused, his green eyes meeting hers. "What's wrong?" he asked softly.

Xanthe took a shaky breath. "I... I don't know if I can do this. It feels so real, but I know it can't be. You're..." She couldn't bring herself to say the word.

Ash's expression softened. He gently cupped her face in his hands. "I know. But we're here now, in this moment. Does it matter if it's real or not?"

Xanthe closed her eyes, leaning into him for a moment. "It matters because when this ends, I'll have to lose you all over again. And I don't know if I can bear that."

"Then don't think about it ending." His voice hardened suddenly. "The Host has given us this gift. Why question it?"

Xanthe looked up at him. As she studied his face, those familiar features she'd memorized over their years together, she saw something else in his eyes. Something she'd never seen before. A coldness. The Host's words echoed in her mind: "Find what you seek."

"You're not him," she whispered, pulling away.

His smile remained, but it was different now.

"Xanthe, you're being paranoid. Come here."

Xanthe took another step back, her heart pounding. "No. You're not Ash. You're... something else."

The thing wearing Ash's face tilted its head, its smile fading. "I am what you wanted, Xanthe. I am the Ash you remember, the one you long for. Why resist?"

"Because it's not real," Xanthe said, her voice growing

stronger. "And Ash... the real Ash... he would want me to face reality, not hide in a fantasy."

The creature's face flickered, Ash's features momentarily replaced by something inhuman. "But reality is pain. Here, you can have everything you've lost."

Xanthe shook her head, backing away toward the door. "No. This isn't what I want. I want to remember Ash as he was, not as some... illusion."

The room around them began to shimmer and fade. Xanthe could hear distant music, the sounds of the ballroom seeping back in.

"You're making a mistake," the creature said, its voice no longer Ash's. "You could stay here forever, in perfect happiness."

As the cabin and the mountain scene around her flickered, Xanthe backed away. The idyllic mountains were dissolving around her, replaced by the shimmering walls of the ballroom.

"No," Xanthe said firmly, her voice growing stronger. "This isn't happiness. It's a lie. And Ash would never want me to live a lie."

The creature's form flickered, its features twisting into something inhuman before settling back into Ash's familiar face. But the eyes were cold now, devoid of the warmth and love that had always defined Ash.

The ballroom solidified around her as the last vestiges of the cabin faded away. The creature snarled, its form becoming increasingly unstable.

"You could have everything you ever wanted," it hissed as it crept toward her.

"Everything I wanted?" Xanthe asked, her voice trembling.. "What I want is to honor Ash's memory, not replace it with a lie. He would have wanted me to live, truly live, not hide in a fantasy."

The Host's form flickered again, its features twisting into something grotesque before settling back into a semblance of humanity. Its eyes, however, remained cold and alien.

Xanthe glanced around the ballroom. The chaos had subsided, replaced by an eerie stillness. The other guests were all gone. The walls around her still flickered in and out and shimmered in the vastness of the now empty room.

"Where is everyone?" Xanthe asked.

"They've accepted what I offer," a voice said simply. "Do you see?"

A line of ballroom dancers filed out from the darkness all around her once again. Xanthe spun wildly around as she tried to take in the scene, the dancers all moving quickly as they paired up.

"Beautiful, isn't it?" The Host's voice came from everywhere and nowhere, his voice getting stronger in their presence. "They've found what they sought. No more pain, no more longing."

But Xanthe saw the truth now. The Host wasn't giving them peace – it was feeding on their grief, their love, their desperation.

Through the haze of movement, she saw William, his eyes fixed in fear as he waltzed around her. Xanthe's heart sank as she watched him dance by, his eyes wide with fear but his body moving in perfect time. She scanned the other faces, recognizing Amara among them, her expression blank as she twirled past.

"This isn't what they wanted," Xanthe said, her voice rising in desperation. "Stop this," she then demanded, turning back to the Host. "Let them go!"

"But why would I do that? Their grief, their longing – it sustains me. And you, Xanthe, you could have joined them. You still can."

Xanthe felt a wave of revulsion wash over her. The true nature of this place, of the Host, was becoming clear. This wasn't a gift or a chance for closure – it was a trap, designed to feed on their most desperate desires and deepest griefs.

"No," Xanthe said, defiantly. "I won't join them, and I won't let you keep them either."

"You have no power here. This is my domain."

But Xanthe stood her ground, her mind racing. There had to be a way to break this spell, to free the others. She thought of Ash – the real Ash, not the hollow imitation the Host had conjured - and what he would do in this situation.

"You're wrong," Xanthe said, her voice steady. "We all have power here because this place, this illusion, it's built on our memories, our emotions. Without us, you have nothing." She turned to the dancers, focusing on William's terrified face as he spun past. "William!" she called out. "Remember why you came here. You wanted to see your family again, but not like this. They wouldn't want you trapped in an illusion!"

William's eyes flickered with recognition but continued his dance.

Xanthe turned and saw Amara. "Amara! Please, this isn't really Zara, she wouldn't want you to waste your life like this!"

Amara kept dancing, her eyes fixed ahead on images only she could see.

"It seems they've made their choice." The Host's voice sounded like a whisper in her ear and in a blink, the dancers were gone.

Xanthe spun around, her heart pounding as she searched the

now-empty ballroom.

"What have you done with them?" she demanded, her voice echoing in the vast space.

"They're simply where they want to be," the host said, its voice clear and strong now.

Xanthe felt a pull in her chest, a longing so deep it threatened to overwhelm her. For a moment, she wavered, the memory of Ash's arms around her, his lips on hers, still fresh in her mind. But with an effort, she pushed the feeling away.

"No," she said firmly. "They may have made their choice, but so have I."

"Then, so be it," the host said with finality .

The ballroom started to crumble, the shimmering walls giving way to an inky void. Xanthe felt the floor beneath her starting dissolve. Panic rose in her chest as she realized she was sinking into nothingness, desperately trying to find something solid to hold onto.

"You could have had everything," the Host's voice echoed all around her. "Now you'll have nothing."

The darkness pressed in on all sides, suffocating and disorienting. Xanthe couldn't tell which way was up or down, couldn't see or feel anything solid.

She thought of Ash, of the life they had shared, of the future they had planned together. She thought of the invitation that had brought her here, of William and Amara, and all the others who had been trapped by their own grief and longing.

As she fell, memories flashed before her eyes – Ash's smile, their first kiss, the day he'd proposed. But mixed with the happy memories were the painful ones – the diagnosis, the long nights in the hospital, the funeral. All of it, the joy and the pain, was part of who she was. It was her story, her life, and she wasn't ready to let it go.

Pinpricks of light began to appear in the darkness around her. They grew brighter, coalescing into familiar shapes – the stars that she and Ash used to gaze at together in the midnight blue sky. The constellations they had mapped out on lazy summer nights came into focus, surrounding her with their gentle light.

The familiar contours of her bedroom slowly came into focus. Xanthe blinked as she took in her surroundings. The dresser with its collection of framed photos, the soft glow of the bedside lamp.

She was lying in her bed, still wearing the midnight blue dress from the ball. She sat up slowly, her head still spinning. Her eyes fell on the framed photo of her and Ash on the nightstand. It was the one from their trip to France, their smiles frozen in a moment of perfect happiness.

She picked up the frame and with a deep breath, walked to the window, pushing it open to let the cool night air wash over her. The stars twinkled overhead, the same stars she and Ash had gazed at together so many times.

"I miss you," she whispered to the night.

# 2

# The Green Man's Toast

*Author's Note*

*I'm very fortunate to live about ten minutes' drive away from one of the most famous and recognizable historic monuments in the world. I say ten minutes' drive, however that's only when there is no other traffic on the road, which is actually never. For those that don't know, the site of Stonehenge sits right by one of the busiest main roads that run through the county of Wiltshire. The road takes visitors all the way to idyllic parts of the counties of Devon and Cornwall in the southwest of England. In the summer months, as many people embark on their summer getaway's, they know they will drive straight past one of the country's most famous sites, so close is it to the road that they won't even need to park to get a great view of it. So, the traffic slows to a crawl as the cameras come out (rather dangerously) to take their moving pictures. All of which makes this otherwise quiet, rural part of Wiltshire one of the most congested parts of the county. That being said, I'm not complaining about my proximity to Stonehenge in any way. I visit the site often with my family and we always enjoy the unique energy and history*

21

*that we experience; experience which never diminishes regardless of how often we visit. It's very easy when you grow used to something so local to grow too accustomed, even cynical toward it.*

*I often have to remind myself how lucky I am to have this historical site so close to me, a site where people have been making pilgrimages for literally thousands of years since its creation. I use the word 'pilgrimage' here deliberately as that's exactly what people still do on the days of the summer and winter solstices. The story of 'The Green Man's Toast' arose after a particularly busy summer solstice. I had just been reading about the Green Man, another great tale in English folklore. He is often depicted as a face surrounded by, or made of, leaves, symbolizing rebirth, growth, and the cycle of life. Associated with nature's vitality and seasonal change, he appears in carvings and stories as a guardian of the natural world, blending pagan and Christian traditions. I felt the tale blended perfectly with what many people seek when they visit Stonehenge and that sometimes, you just need a reminder as to what's really important in life.*

It was dark and Ed's eyes were beginning to droop. He looked at his watch again, trying to make out the position of the hands in what little moonlight there was. 4.20 AM. Five minutes since the last time he looked. With a sigh, he let his arms drop by his sides then wrapped them around his knees. Despite the warm summer night, the grass was cold beneath him. He hadn't thought to bring something to sit on. Most of the people around him were standing now. They chatted excitedly in their small groups. Ed could see some of the Morris dancers were setting up ready for the sunrise, the rhythmical chiming of their bells grating against the largely white noise of the chatter around him. At least it was helping to keep him awake.

He'd come here for a reason, although in this moment, having been sitting here since the previous evening, that reason escaped him. He hoped the thousands of people around him, all of whom had come to the stones for the summer solstice, would give him a sense of togetherness or maybe some vague sense of belonging that he couldn't quite articulate. Now he was here, he couldn't feel it. As they waited for the sun to rise, the groups around him may as well have been on their own planets, all orbiting together but set distinctly apart from his own.

He looked at his watch again. 4.24 AM. Twenty-five minutes or so to go. Then he could finally walk back to his car and get back to his life. He'd lived close to Stonehenge for several years now, and like most people locally, had only really seen the ancient site as he'd driven past it, forced to a snail's pace as everyone else slowed to look at a sight they must've already seen a thousand times in images or on TV. During previous solstices, Ed had made sure to stay away as the hordes descended but even so, he'd always noticed the uptick in visitors. The large campervans parked up, the odd person walking around in long robes and the groups of tourists trying to work out the best form of public transport to the site. Every year, the same comment came from his friends and family – "You should go, you live so close!" – and every year he'd inwardly roll his eyes and respond something like: "Yes, maybe I will one year."

Perhaps it was a misguided attempt to silence their constant prodding, or maybe he'd simply succumbed to years of peer pressure. Whatever the reason, Ed now found himself here, cold, tired, and thoroughly regretting his decision. Stifling yet another yawn, he couldn't help thinking that this whole endeavor had been a colossal waste of time.

Ed shifted uncomfortably, the dew-damp grass now seeping

through his jeans. Through the crowds, he glanced up at the ancient stones. They were impressive in size but looked lifeless and cold to him. Around him, he could hear parts of conversations about ley lines and earth energy as people talked excitedly about their own experiences.

He pulled out his phone, trying to block them out, squinting in the harsh blue light. No signal. Of course. He pulled up his to-do list for tomorrow... no, today. It was a workday; he had several client meetings later, a call with his boss, some invoices to prepare, the usual. A moth fluttered past his face. He swatted it away with an irritated grunt. As he did so, a deep voice chuckled softly beside him.

"They're drawn to the light, you know. They've lived so long with just the moon and the stars, they're not familiar with these new lights. They're curious, I think."

Ed turned to find a man sitting next to him. He hadn't heard anyone approach. The stranger was a lot older than him, his face weathered and with a wild, unkempt beard. He looked at Ed with a soft smile, his eyes a bright, vibrant green which seemed to glow in the pre-dawn light.

"First time at the stones for the solstice?" he asked.

Ed nodded, surprised to find himself answering. "Yeah. I live nearby but never bothered before. To be honest, I'm not sure why I'm here now."

The old man smiled, the corners of his eyes crinkling. "Sometimes, we're called to places without knowing why. The stones have a way of doing that."

Ed glanced down, watching as the man took a sip of something from a small cup. Noticing Ed's look, the man smiled again.

"Don't worry, it's nothing I shouldn't be drinking here. I don't want to be thrown out tonight of all nights!" he said following it with a loud bellowing laugh.

Reaching into a satchel at his side, he pulled out a thermos and another cup. The cup was unlike anything Ed had seen before. Carved from a single piece of rich, dark wood, it sat comfortably in the old man's hand. Ed noticed the intricate leaf and vine carvings which seemed almost alive, twining around the cup's outer circumference. Like the old man himself, that cup seemed to belong here.

"Care to join me? It's a natural brew I make myself. It helps me appreciate the moment. Works even better when it's shared."

Normally, Ed would have declined, but something about the old man's demeanor was comforting. He accepted the cup, inhaling the rich, slightly earthy aroma of the liquid inside.

"Cheers!" the old man offered before raising his cup toward Ed and taking a sip.

Ed raised his own cup with a nod and took a careful sip. It tasted sweet. Of herbs and sunshine.

"I come here every solstice," the old man said, fixing his eyes on the stones. "to celebrate the rebirth of spring, the fullness of summer. To offer a toast to a job well done for another year."

Ed didn't quite understand this last part but took another sip of the sweet drink, nonetheless. "Have you been coming here long?" he asked, not quite knowing what else to say.

The man chuckled softly. "Yes." His smile was wide and warm as he stared at the stones. "Every year things are a little different though. There are more of those now than there used to be." He gestured to the phone in Ed's hand with his cup. "It always amazed me how so many people come here each year, stay up all night through the dark, sometimes in the rain and cold and then when the moment of sunrise finally comes, they watch it through one of those tiny screens."

Ed nodded, realizing he was probably going to do exactly that. Sheepishly, he slipped his phone back into his pocket. The sky was lightening now, transforming from inky black to a softer blue on the horizon. The crowd around them began to stir with anticipation and Ed noticed several TV crews at the periphery, meticulously setting up their equipment. They were rehearsing their shots, preparing to capture the perfect moment when the sun would rise, ready to broadcast to viewers around the world.

People began to jostle slightly for position as the sky lightened further, their exited chatter growing louder by the minute. Phones began to rise, their artificial glow competing with the approaching dawn.

The old man sat quietly next to Ed, his weathered face serene, eyes fixed on the Eastern horizon.

"Look, it's beginning," he murmured softly.

As the first sliver of sun peeked over the horizon, the old man stood and raised his cup. "To the sun, to the earth, to life renewed," he said softly before draining the contents.

Ed found himself standing too, raising his own cup in a toast he didn't fully understand. As he drained the liquid, the sun appeared above the Heel stone, its sudden warmth connecting the earth beneath his feet and the now sapphire blue sky above his head.

For a moment, both Ed and the old man stood in silence, taking in the scene before them. The stones looked different to Ed somehow, the golden light of the rising sun giving them a life he hadn't seen before. Letting out a deep breath, he felt his shoulders relaxing, all thought of the workday ahead gone as he took in everything around him.

"You can keep the cup," the old man said, offering Ed his hand. Ed took it gratefully, feeling the warmth in the old man's grip.

"Maybe I'll see you next year."

With a final wide smile, the man turned and strode away, melting into the crowd and the landscape. Ed watched him go until he was out of sight before glancing down at the cup, his fingers tracing the carved wooden leaves.

"Yes, maybe you will."

# 3

# The Guardian of Willowbrook

***Author's Note***

*At the time of writing this, I'm a parent of two amazing boys. My eldest is ten years old. He's smart, funny, kind, and showing us the kind of person he'll eventually (and much more quickly than I was ever prepared for) grow up to be. My youngest is nearly five years old. He was a Covid-19 baby, born in the early part of 2020, just before the world changed for us all. It was months before he could meet his own grandparents. He's a wonderful boy but approaches the world and the people within it with more trepidation than his outgoing, adventurous brother. As all parents I'm sure will know, it is a daily struggle trying to guide them in the right direction when you feel that you yourself haven't remotely figured things out yet. I know one day we will have to let them go and it's my biggest fear. Selfishly, I want nothing more than to forever be there to protect them, but I won't be. One day, I'll be gone, and they'll have to make their own way in life. It's my job as a parent to give them the best start as I can, to point them in the right direction and then say, "off you go." I then need to trust that when the time comes, they can take care of things themselves. It may be my biggest fear, but watching them now, as the young boys they are, and seeing the hints of the people they will become, gives me the biggest cause for hope as I could ever need.*

Hannah leaned heavily on her oak staff as she made her way back home through the fields of Willowbrook. The golden wheat swayed gently in the breeze, each ear whispering greetings to her as she passed. She'd turned ninety years old this year and even though her steps were slower now, the earth still sang to her, as it had throughout her life.

She paused at the edge of the field and lowered herself to the ground under an old elm tree.

"Yes, old friend, I know," she murmured, placing her palm gently against its rough bark. "Change is coming."

Since she was a young woman, Hannah had been the guardian of this village. Like her mother and her mother's mother before her, she had a connection with the earth. She ensured the sun shone when it needed to, gentle rains fell when required, harsh winds and storms were turned away, and crops flourished year after year. Under her guidance, Willowbrook had known nothing but prosperity and peace for generations.

However, as the autumn leaves were beginning to turn once again, Hannah felt the weight of her years more than ever. Her bones ached with every step and the voices of the earth, once crystal clear, now sometimes faded to whispers.

Rising from the ground, she began making her way toward the village square. She could see the children playing, their faces free from worry. Where once their smiles had brought a sense of pride to Hannah, now they left her feeling uneasy. What would become of them when she was gone, when there was no one in the village to protect them from the harshness of the world?

She had no daughters of her own; the urge had never been strong within her. Finding a partner had never been one of her priorities. She'd always preferred her own company; her connection to the earth was all she needed. The villagers had never thought to question the source of their good fortune.

That night, as Hannah lay in her bed, she felt the roots of the trees and the movements of the clouds, exploring them for any sense of guidance. Hannah rose and walked to her garden. She knelt, pressing her palms to the soil.

"What should I do?" she whispered to the earth. But the earth offered no clear answer.

Nights passed and Hannah's anxiety grew. Each night, as she lay awake, memories of her long life occupied her thoughts. She remembered the challenges she had faced as a young woman, learning to harness her gift. Memories of her own childhood surfaced – her mother letting her fall as she learned to climb trees, standing back as she faced her first storm alone. "You must learn through doing," her mother would say, even as Hannah saw the concern in her eyes.

It hadn't felt like love then, but now Hannah understood. Her mother hadn't sheltered her from failure or pain – she had prepared her for a world that wouldn't always be kind.

Looking at Willowbrook now she was in her twilight years, all pristine and protected, Hannah finally saw what she had done. In trying to be the perfect guardian, she had become an overprotective parent, and her beloved town had grown dependent and fragile. True love meant having the courage to let go, to trust the villagers to find their own way, even if that meant watching them stumble. Like her mother before her,

Hannah would have to find the strength to step back, to let them grow strong through their struggles.

She felt the earth's pulse beneath her, steady and ancient. It had existed long before her, and it would continue long after.

The decision was made. After all these years, it was time. Time to let them go. With a soft sigh, Hannah closed her eyes. With each slow breath, she loosened her hold on the earth around her. The moon still shone, the clouds drifted, and Hannah slept.

# 4

# The Hourglass

**Author's Note**

*The idea for 'The Hourglass' came from my own struggles with writing. For me, as much as I would like it to, the number of words written does correlate directly with the time I have available. I spend a lot of energy inwardly complaining that I don't have enough time to write and then when the time arises, I go ahead and waste it by procrastinating on other things. Like all writers, I'm sure, the only way things get done is by sitting in that chair and doing the work. Time is only part of that equation.*

Jacob sat behind his desk in his dusty old house, tracing his fingers along the delicate features of the silver hourglass. Much like himself, the black sand inside shifted restlessly. How long had it been since he first acquired this cursed object? Decades? Centuries? Jacob had long since forgotten. It didn't matter anymore. Time, for Jacob, was now just an endless stream of stolen moments and of unfulfilled dreams.

Today would be the day it finally ended. Jacob closed his old eyes, remembering the day it had all begun. He had been young once, a writer with an ambition which had burned inside him. Days had never been long enough; there was always too much to do, too much of life taken up by the mundane. When that desperate old man had offered him the hourglass, promising him the gift of time, Jacob thought he'd found the answers to all his problems.

"Turn the hourglass," the man had said, "and you'll have all the time you want!"

At first it was exhilarating. Choosing first to take the remaining time of an elderly man he'd known was already sick. What harm could it do? This man had lived his life already. He turned the hourglass, feeling the rush of stolen time flooding his veins. He wrote feverishly; his masterpiece was just within reach. But it was never enough. He always needed more.

So, he'd turned the hourglass again, and again, and again, the size of his dream and his ambition growing each time he did. Days bled into weeks, weeks into years. Jacob watched the world change around him, watched loved ones wither and die while he remained. And still, his masterpiece eluded him.

The addiction grew. He needed more time, more life to pour into his work. He rationalized it – what were a few years taken from strangers compared to the gift his art would give the world?

But with each turn, the weight of stolen dreams pressed down on him, as if Death itself was fighting back. He began to see them – flashes of lives unlived, aspirations snuffed out. The guilt began to press.

And Jacob's own dreams? They grew monstrous, swelling beyond any hope of achievement. The world's expectations magnified in his mind until every word he wrote felt pathetically inadequate.

33

He tried to stop but the hunger always returned. The need to turn the hourglass one more time. Just one more stolen lifetime and then he'd stop.

Decades passed and still Jacob turned the hourglass.

Until today.

All those years, those centuries of striving, and what did he have to show for it? A dusty house filled with relics of a world long past, and a manuscript that would never be finished. He'd sacrificed everything – his loved ones, his morality, his very soul – for a dream that now meant nothing to him.

Whenever he gazed at his reflection in the tarnished mirror across the room, the face that stared back was a stranger's: wrinkled, hollow-eyed, devoid of the passion that had once driven him. This wasn't living; this was existing in a state of dissatisfaction, always reaching for a perfection that remained tantalizingly out of reach.

The irony wasn't lost on him. He'd stolen time to create something timeless, only to find himself trapped in an endless loop of frustration and regret. The masterpiece he'd envisioned had become a millstone, dragging him down by the neck into the depths of despair.

The idea had seeped up through his consciousness gradually, although he realized now that it had probably been with him for many years. What if he turned the hourglass on himself? The guilt of countless lives cut short, the burden of unfulfilled potential – all of it could be laid to rest.

His eyes fell on the hourglass again, its black sand shifting restlessly. With trembling hands, he lifted it. For a moment, he hesitated. What would happen to all the stolen time when he was gone? Would it return to those he'd taken it from, or dissipate into the ether? He realized it didn't matter. Whatever happened, it would no longer be his burden to bear.

Jacob's gaze swept across the room, taking in what little he had to show for his impossibly long life. Shelves upon shelves of books he'd collected over the centuries. Each item held a memory, a fragment of the life he'd stretched beyond recognition. There were no photographs, no friends or family, or children.

His eyes finally settled on the manuscript, the supposed masterpiece that had driven him to this point. Yellowed pages filled with words that no longer held meaning, dreams that had twisted into nightmares. He realized now that his true story wasn't in those pages, but in the lives he'd touched – and destroyed – along the way.

This ending, he thought, was perhaps the only fitting conclusion to his tale. He would return to the cycle of life and death he'd so long evaded. In his final act, he would embrace the very mortality he'd spent lifetimes running from.

Jacob closed his eyes and turned the hourglass. He felt the familiar rush, but this time, instead of invigorating him, he felt his life force ebbing away. As consciousness began to fade, he felt his body begin to crumble. Ash and dust swirling in that dead room with the hourglass at its center.

Then it was over. The hourglass landed softly on the carpet. Its time was replenished once more. The black sand continued to shift, undisturbed, waiting for the next hand to grasp it, the next dream to devour.

# 5

# Midnight

**Author's Note**

*This might be controversial, but I don't really like cats. I find them distant and cold and not the companions that dogs are. That's just from my perspective as a pet owner though. What I admire cats for is their adventurous nature. Cats sometimes disappear for days, the 'missing' signs go up around town and when all hope seems to be lost, they stroll right back in the house wondering what all the fuss was about. I'd love to ask them where they've been and what adventures they've had, I'm sure the tales they'd be able to tell would be remarkable.*

*It was with this in mind that I wrote the title piece for this collection. I'd recently been on a trip to a town called Boscastle in the English county of Cornwall, a place my parents would take me and brother to every summer when we were kids. It's a gloriously old fishing village on the rugged north coast of Cornwall which, heartbreakingly, was devastated by a freak flash flood in the summer of 2004 where a month's worth of rain fell in a single day, causing two local rivers to burst their banks. Two billion liters of water rushed down the valley, sweeping through the historic village. Mercifully and miraculously, no-one was injured or killed in the disaster but much of the village was damaged or destroyed. In the old harbor, there was a small museum dedicated to Cornish witches and witchcraft which as a child, we never visited. Perhaps it just looked a bit too scary for young Alex. Thankfully, the museum, along with the rest of Boscastle was lovingly repaired and rebuilt following the flood, so this year, I wanted to take my own kids who are far less scared of such things as I was. The museum was wonderful, and I highly recommend you visit if you can. It left me wanting to write stories of witches for which England has a rich folklore.*

Midnight stretched lazily on the windowsill, making sure to conserve as much energy as possible while absorbing the last warm rays of the setting sun. His golden eyes followed the frantic movements of his witch, Morgan, as she hurried around their small living space. As usual, the air was thick with incense, a familiar comfort that usually lulled Midnight into a peaceful sleep.

Tonight was a little different. Tonight, Morgan was on edge and Midnight could feel it. Morgan had spent the evening brewing, and while Midnight had no idea what the potion was, he could still smell it in the air, something dark and acrid mixed with the usually sweet-smelling incense. He watched as Morgan pulled on her deep purple cloak – the one reserved for coven meetings.

"Be good, Midnight," Morgan whispered, scratching behind his ears. "I'll be back in the morning."

Midnight purred instinctively at her touch, even as anxiety gnawed at his insides. He'd been Morgan's familiar for years, bound by magic. But lately, something had felt different. The coven meetings had become more frequent, more secretive. In the past, Morgan had often taken him along where he'd sit with the other familiars, listening idly to their chatter. Not anymore though.

Midnight had been forming a plan for weeks and as soon as the door clicked shut, he leapt from the windowsill onto the cold stone floor. It was time to investigate.

As usual the door had been sealed, but Midnight had his own ways to come and go as he pleased. He was a witch's familiar after all. His golden eyes pierced the shadows in the early evening sun as he made his way to the old theater where the coven met. The abandoned building loomed before him, its façade crumbling and covered in ivy.

Midnight crept through one of the broken windows, his movements slow and silky, and followed the sound of voices. In the middle of the old auditorium, seven witches sat in a circle, a candle flickering in front of each of them. Morgan was among them, her face stern. As he had suspected, none of the other familiars were here.

Midnight approached the circle carefully. They couldn't know he was here. He saw Magda, the oldest of the coven, speaking at the top of the circle. Her face was covered in its usual dark red veil. Without making a sound, he inched closer, close enough so he could hear what they were discussing.

"...the seven of us will finally gain what we've been working toward for all these years."

Midnight raised his ears to their fullest, straining to hear more. Morgan was speaking now.

"...the brew is progressing. It should be ready for tomorrow night. There is plenty of it for us all."

"What is its potency?" Magda asked, her face slowly turning in Morgan's direction.

"It is strong," Morgan replied, her face impassive.

"If we are as strong, The Night Spell should take no more than an hour to complete."

"And what of our familiars?" another witch asked. From her voice, Midnight guessed it was Samantha, one of the younger witches of the coven.

"They are magical creatures, they will survive," Magda replied dismissively. "The spell takes only from the non-magical."

Midnight crouched lower in the darkness, half closing his golden eyes as Magda rose to her feet, the other witches following suit.

"Tomorrow then, my friends. And when The Night Spell is completed and there is nothing non-magical left of this place, we will move on with youth and with power."

Midnight felt the hairs on his tail stand on end and his back arched as if the words themselves might harm him. This was wrong. He had to do something, but what? He was bound to the witch who seemed intent on casting this terrible spell.

He slipped away, the sounds of the coven's chanting ringing in his ears. Where should he go? Athena, she'd hear him out. He didn't have long though; the coven meeting would be over soon, and Morgan would expect him to be at home.

*The oak tree, that's where to start, she'll be there, watching*, he thought.

Midnight ran as fast as he could, squeezing back through the hole in the broken window and hurrying out into the night. The huge, ancient oak in the park was easy to see from all around and as he approached, a soft, familiar hooting drew his golden eyes upward.

39

"Well, well," came a voice like wind through leaves. "What brings Morgan's shadow to my tree?"

Athena was perched on one of the upper branches. She was a tawny owl with eyes almost as bright as Midnight's. Samantha's familiar.

"Athena, please, we need to talk, quickly!" Midnight pleaded. He knew they didn't have long. Athena would be keeping an eye on the coven from here and would know when the meeting was over.

"You know I can't come down," she replied haughtily. "If you want to speak with me, you'll have to climb up here." She turned her head away from him.

Midnight sighed. He didn't have time for this but there was no choice; he knew Athena would not be swayed. He started climbing, claws digging into the rough bark of the ancient oak, his dark fur shaking with the effort. An amused Athena watched his progress from the corners of her eyes.

Finally reaching her high branch, and holding on tightly, Midnight wasted no time in getting to the point.

"Athena, it's the coven, they're going to perform The Night Spell."

Athena ruffled her feathers, all signs of amusement fading from her eyes.

"The Night Spell? A..are you sure?" the owl stuttered, her eyes narrowing.

"Yes, I've just overheard them, they're going to perform the spell tomorrow night. We need to do something."

"You overheard them?" Athena pressed. "You mean you were spying?"

Midnight's nose twitched in frustration. "You must have been feeling it too. We haven't been to a coven meeting for months.

Morgan has been acting distant for weeks, all our witches have, and that brew she's been working on, it's all been in preparation for this."

Athena stared at Midnight, examining him for a moment before she responded.

"Such magic upsets the balance of our world," she answered distantly.

"What can we do?" Midnight implored.

Athena paused, evidently thinking. "Perhaps two familiars aren't enough to stop them. But we're not the only magical creatures in this city, are we?"

With a powerful beat of her wings, she took flight. Midnight scrambled down the tree and raced after her, his black fur blending into the night as he struggled to keep her in sight. They reached the small pond at the center of the park where Athena landed gracefully and silently on the branch of an overhanging tree.

"Melusine," Athena called softly. "Are you there?"

At her words, the water's surface shimmered and rippled. Midnight watched as a delicate, fluid face began to form.

"Athena, wise one," Melusine's voice sang. "And Midnight, the shadow-walker. What brings you to my banks?"

Once again, Midnight recounted what he'd heard in the coven meeting. Melusine's watery features darkened like a storm cloud.

"This cannot come to pass," she said, her voice like rapids over rocks. "The balance must be maintained. I will help you."

"Thank you, Melusine," Athena said softly.

Midnight's tail twitched anxiously. "Who else can we turn to? The coven meeting will be ending soon."

Athena's eyes gleamed. "There is one more who could help

41

us."

"Who?" Midnight asked.

"We need to find Kitsune," Athena said simply.

Melusine's watery form rippled. "Kitsune? The shape-shifting fox? I've heard of her trickery. Are we sure she can be trusted with this?"

"It's worth a try, her abilities are powerful, and this threat may be grave enough to rouse her interest."

Midnight looked toward the forest on the outskirts of the park. "How do we find her?"

"I'm pretty sure she's already listening," Athena said with a chuckle.

"You know me too well, Athena!" a high voice said from the darkness behind them.

Midnight, jumped at the sound, the fur on his back standing upright.

"Then you'll already know what we want to ask of you, Kitsune," Athena responded, the calm in her features unwavering.

"Yes, The Night Spell," Kitsune said, shaking her head. "A tough one, but maybe it's what the world needs?"

"You don't mean that!" Midnight shouted. "You must help us stop them; you know this is wrong!"

"Perhaps," Kitsune said airily, turning and strolling back toward the forest, her multiple tails swaying hypnotically. "I'll think about it."

~

The next day, Midnight was restless. Every instinct screamed at him to warn Morgan, to make her understand that what she was about to do was wrong, but he knew it wouldn't work. Her face was set. With every passing hour, she became more manic as she prepared for the meeting that night. Before sunset, Midnight crept out and made his way back to the ancient oak tree where the four familiars had agreed to meet.

"Where is Kitsune?" Midnight asked, failing to keep the note of panic from his voice.

"It would seem we may have to do this without her," Athena sighed. "She was never reliable, but it was worth a try."

Midnight took a deep, calming breath, trying to suppress the disappointment and anger he felt at Kitsune's absence. Together, they made their way back to the old theater and waited.

As darkness fell, they watched as the seven witches came together. Morgan was there in her dark purple robe, taking her place in the circle at the center of which stood a large cauldron. As one, they began to chant, their voices coming together in a haunting harmony.

Midnight glanced at Athena and could see his own trepidation reflected in her large eyes. It was time their plan sprang into action. With a final nod she took flight and Midnight watched as she began to swoop around the large auditorium, her wings spread wide, emitting an ear-piercing screech which rang around the empty, cavernous room. The chanting stopped as the witches covered their ears, desperately trying to block out the terrible noise.

Melusine's voice suddenly rose above the chaos, summoning a thick mist that rolled through the room. Midnight knew it was his turn now. Keeping his golden eyes fixed on center of the circle, he darted quickly and silently through the mist toward the cauldron. But then Magda's voice rose above them all, strong and terrible. The other witches rallied, their voices joining hers as the mist began to lift. He was so nearly there when he felt a rough hand grab him by the fur and lift him up into the air.

"Midnight, what are you doing?" Morgan scowled.

Midnight watched in horror as a dark, swirling cloud began to form above them, the acrid smell he was so familiar with filling his senses. They'd failed. The spell was happening.

A movement suddenly caught his eye at the center of the circle. With wide-eyed shock, he saw what looked like himself stroll slowly and purposefully toward the cauldron. The other cat's golden eyes shining in the pulses of light emanating from the dark cloud above. Lazily, it placed a single paw against the cauldron and pushed.

"No!" the witches cried in unison as the brew gushed out across the floor. It's dark liquid burning the carpet of the old theater as the cauldron emptied.

Together, the witches fell to their knees. Above them, the cloud they had summoned loomed ominously, its edges swirling with power. With a final, piercing, the cloud descended toward them, enveloping them in its all-encompassing darkness. And just like that, the cloud and the witches were gone.

The room was empty once more. Midnight looked above and saw Athena circling before looking back toward the cauldron, now empty and lying on its side.

"You helped us after all."

The dark-furred cat turned its golden eyes on Midnight, its form shimmering slightly. With a mischievous glint in its eye, the cat's shape began to change, elongating into the familiar form, its seven tails flowing behind.

"I couldn't let you have all the fun, now could I?" Kitsune said, her voice light and playful.

"What happens now?" Midnight asked, gazing at the spot

where Morgan once stood, tears now filling his eyes.

"Well, that's entirely up to you," Kitsune said, as Athena landed softly beside them. "I'm sure you'll both think of something."

# 6

# Melusine

**Author's Note**

*As you have just read, Melusine originally appeared in my story 'Midnight'. While I would love to take credit for the character, she is actually rooted in European folklore, often depicted as a woman who transforms into a serpent or mermaid-like creature from the waist down on certain days. She marries a mortal man, typically under the condition that he never sees her in her transformed state. When her husband inevitably breaks this taboo, he loses her forever as she returns to her supernatural origins. Melusine is a symbol of duality, blending human and otherworldly qualities, and is associated with themes of love, betrayal, and the mysterious power of nature. The tale originates from medieval France, particularly in the Poitou region, but variations of the story have spread across Western Europe where she'd sometimes be depicted as a water spirit or shapeshifter of some kind. In the story you're about to read, I wanted to consider the themes of betrayal and love but from conflicting perspectives. As children, we always felt like we knew better than our sometimes more jaded parents. How would Melusine's child react to the news of her father's betrayal toward her mother, and how would her worldview change in the face of her own new experience of feeling loved?*

Sarah sat at the edge of the weathered dock as the moon cast silver light across the lake, her bare feet brushing the surface of the water. She didn't dare breathe as Michael leaned in, his breath warm against her face. Their lips met. The lake rippled in front of her, but Sarah saw nothing of it as the world around her faded.

As Michael pulled away, Sarah opened her eyes, slowly, as if waking from a dream.

"I should go," Michael whispered, his voice cracking slightly. "See you tomorrow?"

Sarah nodded. She didn't quite trust herself to form words just yet. She watched him walk away, back down the path through the forest, his silhouette blending into the shadows of the trees that surrounded the lake house. When he was gone, she turned back to the lake, allowing herself to breathe at last.

The surface broke.

A woman emerged from the deep, water flowing across her dark hair as her pale face and shoulders rose from the inky water.

Sarah scrambled backward, pulling her feet quickly away from the water's surface.

"What... who are you?" Sarah stammered; her eyes wide in shock at the apparition in front of her.

The woman stared at Sarah for a moment, the water matting her long, dark hair around her face and shoulders like seaweed, glistening in the early evening moonlight. When she finally spoke, her voice was soft like the watery ripples around her.

"My name is Melusine. I am your mother."

Sarah stared at her in disbelief, unable to move further. She then shook her head slowly.

"No. That's impossible. My mother died when I was a baby."

Melusine moved slowly but purposefully toward until she was level with the dock, her dark eyes never leaving Sarah's.

"A lie. Told by your father no doubt."

"You're not real," Sarah insisted as Melusine rose gracefully from the water and took a seat on the dock in front of her.

Melusine reached out a hand, water dripping from her fingers, a sad smile on her lips.

"Take my hand if you don't believe me," she offered tenderly. "You'll find I'm very real. I've watched you grow from afar for all these years and now you've known love's first kiss, it's time I showed myself to you. To explain the truth."

Sarah hesitated, then slowly extended her hand toward her mother's. Melusine's touch was cool and slick, like polished stone beneath a running stream.

"What truth?" Sarah asked, her voice low and cracked.

Melusine's eyes darkened, like the sky above them.

"To warn you, my daughter. To protect you from the fate that befell me. Your father was not the man you think he was," Melusine continued, her voice low and hypnotic. "He was charming, but beneath the sweet words was a cold heart."

Sarah listened as Melusine told her tale. Of how she'd fallen in love with a mortal man, how she'd trusted him with her heart and her secrets. How he'd betrayed her, using her power for his own gain and exposing her true nature to the world.

"He swore to keep my secret," Melusine said, her voice heavy with pain. "But promises are as fragile as reflections on water. One careless word, one moment of weakness, and everything is gone."

Sarah thought of Michael, of his warm smile and gentle touch.

"But not all men are like that," she protested. "Michael would never –"

Melusine's laugh was bitter. "They all say that. Every young girl believes her love is different, special. They are not."

"You're wrong," Sarah said, anger flaring, the feeling of the kiss still so real on her lips. "You don't know Michael. You don't know me!"

"I know the pain of betrayal," Melusine countered, her eyes flashing. "I know the agony of watching the man I love desert me. I've spent years alone, bound to this lake, all because I dared to love a mortal man."

Sarah stood, her fists clenched.

"Is that why you abandoned me? Left me to grow up without a mother? Because you were afraid?"

Melusine recoiled. "I never abandoned you. I've watched over you every day of your life. But the curse..."

"Curse?" Sarah scoffed. "The only curse I see is the one you've placed on yourself. Hiding away, bitter and alone, too scared to trust anyone."

"You don't understand," Melusine pleaded, reaching for her daughter. "I'm trying to protect you."

Sarah stepped back, shaking her head. "No, you're trying to control me. To make me as miserable and distrustful as you are. Well, I won't let you. I'm not afraid to love, even if it means risking getting hurt."

"My daughter, please." Melusine began.

"No," Sarah said simply, turning back toward the house. "You know nothing of me. You are not my mother."

Sarah's feet pounded against the rocky path as she stormed

back to the lake house, her fists clenched, and teeth gritted. She couldn't believe her moment with Michael, the moment she'd been waiting so long for had been ruined.

Stopping at the edge of the porch, she turned and gazed back at the now-calm lake. Even through her anger, she couldn't help but wonder why her mother had hidden from her for so long. Was it really true? Had her father really kept this secret from her for all these years?

Sarah pushed open the wooden door and climbed the stairs to her bedroom, each step slower than the last. Through her window, the lake gleamed silver in the moonlight, its surface now still and unbroken, just like she'd always known it. She glanced down at her hand, still cool and damp from her mother's touch, as if Melusine still held it. The sensation lingered, as real as the memory of Michael's kiss. Sarah held them both tightly.

# 7

# The Vanishing at Northcott Mouth

*Author's Note*

*I'm sure by now, you will have gained a sense of how important the southwest of England is to me. I grew up in London and spent my first eighteen years surrounded by people and traffic. In the subsequent twenty or so years, I've moved further and further away and am now settled in Wiltshire with my young family. I never minded London. It's arguably the beating heart of the United Kingdom but I never felt at home there. It felt, and still feels, somewhat soulless to me.*

*As a child, we'd often take trips out to the southwest during breaks in school time. We'd often go to Bude, a town on the north coast of Cornwall. It has a rich history but is now also known for its surfing culture. We'd take walks along the coastal cliffs and spending time on its wide sandy beaches. I wanted to do something a little different with this story. I'd been thinking about the north coast of Cornwall and its seafaring history, and I settled on a format of a missing person's case file entry. And yes, it involves mermaids.*

CASE FILE # 914d3e5bk0f
  MISSING PERSON: Nate Trewin
  STATUS: OPEN
  Evidence Item #4:
  Personal Diary Retrieved from: Breakwater Rd, Bude, EX23
  Date of Recovery: August 28, 2024

Notes: The following pages were found in a waterproof notebook in the subject's home office. The entries detail the subject's alleged encounters with what he describes as a 'mermaid' in the weeks leading up to his disappearance. Family members report the subject had been behaving erratically and spending unusual amounts of time at local beaches. Last known sighting was on August 25, 2024, near Northcott Mouth by local dog walker, Ian Hawken. Investigation ongoing.

~

—– START OF DIARY ENTRIES —–

August 15th, 2024

*I know it sounds mad, but I saw a mermaid today. I was running along the breakwater at Summerleaze beach this evening. The tide was out but all the tourists were gone and that's when I saw her, perched on top of Barrel Rock. At first, I thought she was a seal but when she turned to look at me and the sun behind her reflected back from that tail, I knew! I ran as far as I could toward where she sat but as I got closer she vanished. No one is going to believe me, so I have to write this down. I'll go back tomorrow; she must be out there somewhere.*

~

August 16th, 2024

*I went out to the breakwater again tonight but no sign of her. I waited until the sun was almost gone but no luck. I'll try again tomorrow and maybe venture further, maybe past the sea pool to middle beach. Perhaps I scared her off last night.*

~

August 19th, 2024

*I've been out looking at the beach every night since but still nothing. I think some locals are starting to become concerned about me as I saw some pointing tonight. I know what I saw. I started sketching her today. It helps somehow. Helps me hold on to her. Tomorrow I'll widen my search out to Crooklets Beach. I know she's there somewhere. I can feel her watching me.*

~

August 22nd, 2024

*I haven't slept in days. Every time I close my eyes, I see her. It's maddening. I've taken to swimming out past the breakers at night, hoping I can go to her instead. My wife thinks I'm having a breakdown. Maybe I am. I tell her I can't sleep, and I need the fresh air, but I know she doesn't believe me. I don't care. I have to find her.*

~

August 25th, 2024

*That dog walker! That dog walker! It was at Northcott Mouth, just as the sun was rising. I'd been there all night. Just as the sky was starting to turn pink I saw her head rise from the water maybe 50 meters out to sea. She was looking at me! All around me I could hear her song. It was flowing through me. I ran and threw myself into the water. It was cold, but I didn't care. I swam toward her. Her song was so loud! Then she was there, right in front of me. Her hands were on my face. I tasted the salt on her lips, felt her cold, smooth skin against mine.*

*Then that dog walker. He shouted and she slipped away. Gone. I screamed until my throat was raw. I still feel her, still hear her. I need her. All of her. No distractions, just us.*

*Tomorrow. Tomorrow I'll be hers. In her world. Where I belong.*

# 8

# Shades of Doubt

*Author's Note*

*This is another story where I wanted to play around with the format. At first, I thought that maybe this would work well written as a screenplay, given that the two characters involved were an interviewer and interviewee, however I ultimately settled on a slightly different approach where the story is presented as a transcription of an interview as I liked the fact it gave a little more mystery to things.*

*Warnings: Adult Themes*

The following is a transcription of a lost video recording obtained by this publication, following the suicide of senior writer, Simon Graves.

*Graves:* Mr. Gale, thanks for coming in. May I call you James?

*Gale (restless):* Yes, yes of course, thanks for having me, yes.

*Graves:* So, James, can you tell our readers why you reached out to us?

*Gale (fidgeting):* Well, the police wouldn't listen. They said I was drunk or on drugs or something, but I'm telling you, she took it from me.

*Graves:* Took what exactly?

*Gale:* My shadow. She stole my goddamned shadow.

*Graves:* Your shadow?

*Gale:* Yes, my shadow. (*He stands, gesturing at the floor*) See? Nothing!

*Graves:* James, the lighting in here...

*Gale (interrupting):*It's not the lighting! It's gone, she took it!

*Graves:* Please James, calm down. Why don't you start from the beginning.

*Gale (sits back down, takes a deep breath):* I met her at the Wellington a few nights ago. Stunning woman. Long, jet black hair. Really big brown eyes. I'd never seen anyone like her.

*Graves:* OK...

*Gale:* Well, we started talking, had a few drinks and after a while, she invited me back to hers.

*Graves:* And you went?

*Gale:* Well, yeah...of course I went, wouldn't you!

*Graves:* And what happened?

*Gale:* We... you know. It was really intense, like nothing I've ever experienced. It was like she became someone different.

*Graves:* Different, how?

*Gale:* Well, during... what we were doing,she kept chanting. It was almost like I didn't need to be there after a while. She was in her own world. She just kept getting louder and louder until... well... you know. That's when I think she did it.

*Graves:* Stole your shadow?

*Gale (nods vigorously)*:Yes! I didn't notice anything to start with. When I woke up, she was gone. She'd left me alone at hers which I thought was strange, so I got dressed and left. That's when I noticed. When I went outside.

*Graves:* Mr. Gale, you understand how this sounds right? Shadows aren't tangible things. They can't be stolen.

*Gale:* (*leans toward, intense*): That's what I thought. But she did it. She's a witch or something!

*Graves:* Have you considered that maybe...

*Gale (suddenly standing):* I knew it, you don't believe me either!

*Graves:* No, no, I do! But you did say you'd had a few drinks?

*Gale (pulling the curtains open):* I'll prove it to you! Look!

*Graves (gasps):* How... how did you do that?

*Gale:* I told you already. I didn't do anything. She did. The witch did this to me.

*Graves (standing):* Mr. Gale, I think we need to end this interview.

*Gale (voice rising):*Wait! You have to help me! You have to tell people!

*Graves (backing away):*I'm sorry. I need to go. Thank you for your time.

*(Sounds of footsteps, a door opening and closing)*

*Gale:* Wait! Come back! You have to tell everyone... you have to... (sighs)

*(A shadow moves)*

*Gale (closes eyes, whispers, voice now feminine):* He won't tell anyone about me, I'll make sure of it. You don't need to run from me, my love. I told you before, I'll take care of you.

# 9

# The Twilight Sorrow

*Author's Note*

*It's always been pretty clear to me why the sea has inspired so much folklore around the world. For any seafarer from any age, its vastness must have been terrifying. In the UK, we're surrounded by ocean but not all ocean is created equal. We have the North Sea to the east, the Irish Sea to the west, the English Channel to the south and the wild Atlantic in the south west. Each have a distinctive personality which imposes itself on the coastline of the UK. 'The Twilight Sorrow' arose from reading about Cornish smugglers and Pirates. The north Cornish coast is wild and rugged making it the perfect place historically for smugglers to hide. The risk was significant however and parts of this coastline have been responsible for a large number of shipwrecks. I wanted to evoke this sense of mystery in this story and show that maybe there is more out there than we know.*

The water hit Jack like a cannon ball. His head throbbed, the taste of salt and rum thick on his tongue. Rubbing his eyes from the assault of water and light, he slowly started to focus on his unfamiliar surroundings – a ship's hold, but not a vessel he remembered boarding.

"Get up, lad," a gravelly voice called. "Captain wants all hands on deck."

Jack instinctively scrambled to his feet, following the hunched figure up the ladder. The deck was shrouded in mist, the wood beneath his feet Grey and weathered. Around him, crew members moved quickly about their duties, their forms flickering like sunlight reflecting off the waves.

"I don't understand," Jack stammered. "Where am I?"

The old man who'd woken him cackled, his laugh splintering the air around them.

"You're aboard the *Twilight Sorrow*, lad. Don't you remember signing on?"

Jack furrowed his brow as he tried to force the memories back. He remembered a tavern, a game of cards. His hand sprang to his face as he felt the pain and swelling around his left eye. Yes, there had been a brawl, something about cheating, and then, nothing.

"I... I don't remember signing on to any ship," Jack muttered.

The old sailor's eyes glinted. His smile widened.

"No. No one ever does," he said simply.

Jack stumbled across the deck behind the old man, his legs unsteady beneath him. The mist swirled around his ankles, thick and cold. He reached out to steady himself against the ship's rail; it felt wrong somehow, like smoke beneath his fingers.

*A flash of memory – a tavern door swinging open, a gust of salty air.*

"Best get your sea legs quick, lad," the old sailor called out, noticing Jack's unease. "The Captain don't carry passengers!"

Jack blinked, trying to focus on the crew around him. Their movements were fluid on the rolling deck. Some seemed to fade in and out of view as they worked, their edges blurring into the mist.

*Laughter echoing in his ears, the clink of coins on a worn wooden table. A stranger's voice, low and enticing. "One last game? Winner takes all."*

"You! Check the rigging!" a voice called from above. Jack looked up to see a figure balanced impossibly on the highest yardarm, its form translucent against the Grey sky. With a sinking feeling, he realized the figure was pointing at him.

Swallowing hard, Jack made his way to the main mast. His hands grasped the ropes, but they felt insubstantial, as if woven from sea foam rather than hemp.

*The feeling of cards in his hands, edges worn smooth by countless games. The stranger's eyes, dark and fathomless as the ocean. "Are you sure you want to bet everything, boy?"*

As he climbed, the air grew colder. The ship below seemed to stretch and distort, the distance to the deck growing impossibly vast. Jack closed his eyes, fighting a wave of vertigo.

"Open your eyes, boy," the old man's voice shouted.

Jack's eyes snapped open. He found himself back on the deck, the old sailor watching him with an amused grin.

*A final hand of cards laid out on the table. The stranger's smile, revealing teeth sharp as a shark's. "Looks like I win."*

Jack looked down at his hands, seeing the misty air moving through them.

"I... I lost a bet?" he whispered, the memory trickling back.

The old sailor nodded solemnly. "Aye, lad. That you did."

*A fist swinging through the air, missing. It was Jack's. His head knocked back. Pain around his eye. Then the glint of a blade coming toward him.*

Jack remembered the stranger's eyes now – deep and dark, like ocean itself. How they seemed to look straight through him as he shuffled the deck of cards. The intensity of them, like a storm as he drew his dagger.

"I thought... I thought I could beat him," Jack said, his voice hollow as the realization came to him. "I thought I could win."

"Many have tried, lad," the old sailor said, his voice softening slightly. "Many have tried."

Jack watched as the mists parted over the ocean, revealing an endless expanse of dark, roiling sea. The *Twilight Sorrow* sailed on, carrying its crew toward an eternity of restless voyaging.

Jack turned to the old sailor, a question forming on his lips.

The old man smiled, a mixture of pity and understanding in his eyes. "Aye, lad. You'll be with us for a long time to come."

# 10

# Healing

*Author's Note*

*This is a little different from the other stories in this collection as it's more introspective. Healing from anything is a process that I don't feel ever truly ends; there's no finishing line, no quick fixes, just things that help along the journey. For me, connecting with my inner child regularly is important as it helps with self-care and self-compassion and for someone who is often too hard on themselves, it helps me ground myself and allow my fatherly instincts to point inwards from time to time. While I'm not healing from any major trauma, it's an approach that helps me to stay compassionate toward myself and toward others.*

*Warnings: Childhood trauma*

It had been ten years since Jake had been here but from the outside, nothing had changed. The road was the same, the adjacent houses were the same and despite all that had happened since his time here, the memories remained the same. Walking up to the front door, he could have been a boy again arriving home from school. The same deep anxiety was still there as he tried to calm his breathing. *Time travel really does exist*, he thought.

As he stood facing the old wooden front door, the smell of the old varnish made his heart rate increase, and his palms felt slick with that all too familiar perspiration. He knew the monster wasn't here. It was gone and so now were all its possessions. The last few days of clearing the house had been among st the hardest of his life, but it was done now and after today, he would never have to come here again.

"The last time," he reminded himself, then put the key in the lock and turned it. As the door opened, the faint smell of dust and old cigarette smoke hit him as it had done every time the door had opened this week, bringing the past flooding back to him. Though he knew what was coming, it still pinned him at the threshold. He closed his eyes. "The last time, then no more."

The house was bare, but it felt the same to him as it always had. It was Sam's idea that he come back here again. This time though, she waited outside in the car. This is something he needed to do alone. Since he got the call, the call that confirmed the monster was finally gone, he'd been acting largely on autopilot. His first reaction was surprise. Since cutting ties all those years ago, he'd never expected to be mentioned in the will, let alone be named the sole executor. It seemed he would have to take care of the formalities; the monster forcing its goodbye on him. Dispassionately, he'd arranged the funeral; no one had turned up except him and Sam. Afterwards, financial matters had to be settled. Even as he'd directed the house clearance, as items and furniture he knew from childhood were removed and disposed of, he hadn't allow himself to really see it. Time had just passed and he watched as if he was watching traffic.

This final visit was different through, it had to be. Too much of his life had remained here. The monster still had him, and it was time for it to release its grip. His feet led him to the door of his old room. The action was automatic. It was what he'd always done when he'd come home. His room was his old refuge; he knew he'd find himself here. He opened the door to the now empty space and stood on the patch of flooring next to where his old bed used to be. He looked at the wall opposite for a while then closed his eyes and took some deep breaths. This is what he was here to do.

He could see it all now. It had always been a bare room. Growing up, he'd never had much, just few old books and toys he had outgrown but still cherished. He looked down at the bed and saw his younger self. A small boy in basic clothes, maybe seven or eight years old. His eyes were wet and glistening and Jake could see pale yellows and deeper purples of old and fresh bruising around them. The boy showed no emotion as he looked straight ahead.

"Hi" Jake said to the boy. "I'm sorry it took me so long, but I'm here now." He sank onto the bed and slid his arm around the boy's shoulders. They sat for a while in silence. "I'm here to tell you how proud I am of you. You've done so well. I know the pain and loneliness you're feeling in this room, this house, but it's all going to work out, y'know?"

He wanted to make sure this boy would always know this feeling, this security.

"When you're older, you will escape this place. You'll find the strength to run and never return. You'll learn that the world

65

is not as bad as it seems now, and you'll meet some wonderful people. Your life does not start and end in this house. Some days it will be hard, and you'll find yourself back in this room, reliving these times, but it won't last. I can tell you this for certain because you'll meet a person who will surround you with so much love that it'll push the monster further and further away each day. You'll show your own children what could have been. This place will not hold you anymore."

There was so much more Jake wanted to say to the boy, to reassure him, to let him know he was loved. He wanted him to feel as safe and secure as Sam had made him feel.

An idea came to him. "You know what? Why don't you meet her? Sam, I mean. My girlfriend?" The boy looked up then and with a tentative smile, nodded. "Great! You'll love her, I promise!"

Pulling out his phone, Jake dialed Sam's number.

"Hey, is everything OK?"

"Yes, would you mind coming in? We're upstairs."

"We?"

"You'll see, just come!"

He ended the call. A few moments later, he heard the front door open.

"Up here!" he called. Before Sam entered the room, Jake gave the boy a reassuring smile and winked.

"This is for you," he said softly, "for being so strong. I think it's time we built a new memory of this room."

The door opened and Sam's slender frame entered. Her large brown eyes darted tentatively around the room, a small frown creasing her brow. She'd never been in this house before but knew the effect it had had on Jake even though he rarely spoke about it.

"Hey Sam, do you remember our first dance?"

A confused smile twisted her lips.

"Of course."

"Well, I think we need to recreate it."

"What, here? Now?"

"Yeah, I want to remember this place differently."

"Of course," Sam said, letting out a relieved breath. "I'd love that."

Jake placed his phone on the floor in the middle of the empty room and pressed play. The opening notes of the song that meant so much to them began to play. Jake held out his hand toward Sam, his eyes not leaving hers as they stepped toward each other. He held her tightly as they slowly swayed to the music, breathing in her scent as they moved.

This is how he would remember this house now. The stale cigarette smoke, the yelling, the bruises, all melted away until all he could feel was Sam's arms around him.

When the song was over, Jake held Sam tightly and looked deep into her eyes.

"Let's go home," he said.

# 11

# The Meeting

***Author's note***

*The idea of Angels and Demons on your shoulder isn't new and I'm sure everyone has had this battle with conscience. Sometimes, you make the right decision and sometimes the wrong one. Often, we're not even sure of which is which. Sometimes, we don't know who is speaking, the Angel or the Demon. Ideas of right and wrong are often nuanced, though sometimes they're not. You, like the rest of us, have to decide.*

"He's here, I told you he would be."

"That means nothing. He hasn't done anything wrong by coming to a bar after work."

A busy London bar is the perfect place to be hidden. You become anonymous just by entering. Which is exactly why this place was chosen. At a table somewhere in the front courtyard sit two men. Nobody else notices them. If anyone did however, they'd appear to be another couple of colleagues enjoying an after-work drink in the early evening sunshine. No one saw them enter and no one will see them leave. They're here to settle a wager.

*"He's early too, this will be the best thing he's ever done for himself."*

*"No, he's arrived early so he has time to talk himself out of this."*

A few tables away, a man sits in turmoil. He tries but fails to look casual. Unsure of where to look or what to do with his hands, he pulls out his phone. In recent years, he feels his phone is the only thing that he has truly to himself. The only thing that doesn't belong to anyone else. His other personas live there.

*"Are you getting worried yet? I've been telling you for years that he would end up here eventually. From the very beginning he wasn't happy, he knew it. He tried to convince himself, but he always knew."*

*"No, I'm not worried at all. He's a good person and doesn't want to hurt his family. Everyone in a long-term, committed relationship will have these similar doubts from time to time."*

The man takes a few glances around but knows it's not time yet. They'd agreed to meet at 7. It's 6.45. He reminds himself to breathe. He closes all of his social media feeds and opens his camera roll.

*"He's spent all these years always putting others first, martyring himself in the name of 'honor' and 'integrity'. Well, it's about time, he's finally realized there are no do-overs, you live life once and once only. If you don't experience all life has to offer, surely that's an offense to the privilege of having life itself?"*

The man sitting alone sighs then closes his eyes for two more deep, long breaths. He reopens his social media feeds. There's another message. The man glances at it and then looks quickly away.

*"Let me ask you this: if honesty and integrity are so important,*

*then why does that only apply externally? Why is being honest to your own feelings and desires less important than those of others? When the end comes, is it really a life well lived if you've lived up to everyone else's expectations but ignored yourself? Why do you have to respect others ahead of respecting yourself?"*

He looks at his watch again. 6.50. A short but intense shiver rises in him. He suppresses it with a deep breath.

*"He can do this. No-one else knows he's here and no-one will ever know it's happened. He can go home tomorrow and carry on like nothing out of the ordinary occurred. He was just on a 'work trip'. He takes those all the time. He'll be back in his mundane little world in the morning. No one is hurt, everyone is happy."*

He types out a reply then quickly puts the phone face down on the table.

*"It's not about valuing everyone else's feelings above your own. By living the values of honesty and integrity toward others, you're showing yourself that you can respect yourself in those terms as well."*

6.55. He quickly finishes his drink and wonders if he has time to get another. Something stronger this time.

*"If he does this, even if no-one ever finds out, do you really think no one gets hurt? He's been a good man, done everything he can to help and support everyone he cares for. He takes pride in that. If he goes through with this, it will fundamentally change how he looks at himself. He would be the only one left hurt and he won't be able to turn back the clock."*

6.58. He reopens his camera roll.

*"It's simple really. The reason I'm not worried is because he respects himself too much to do this."*

6.59. He sees a woman approach the courtyard from across the road, searching the faces in front of her. He recognizes her immediately. He gets up, picks up his phone and starts walking in her direction. He makes a call.

"Hey honey, good news, I'm on my way home."

"No, they didn't need me after all."

"No don't wait up for me."

"OK fine. I can bring home my own food."

"OK bye."

Without looking back, the man walks out of the courtyard. The woman, her brow furrowing, keeps searching for the man she'd arranged to meet. The men at the table at the front of the courtyard are gone.

# 12

# Unit 6E

***Author's Note***

*The idea for Unit 6E came to me while thinking about the weight of conformity and the unease that comes with resisting it. There's something deeply unsettling about watching others fall into step with an unseen force, leaving you to stand alone against the pull. What does it take to hold on to yourself when everything else is dragging you toward the same void? I guess this story is about resistance and about holding onto yourself when it would be easier, maybe safer, to give in.*

The storm arrived just as the microwave pinged. Through his sixth-floor window, Ryo watched as lightning illuminated the identical apartment blocks of Kita-Kashiwa, their looming silhouettes stark against the purple-black sky. Thunder followed soon after, causing the lights to flicker once, twice and then die completely.

Ryo stood motionless in his dark apartment, still holding his heated bento. In the sudden silence, the hum of his refrigerator fading to nothing felt oddly final. He placed the food on his counter and fumbled for his phone.

8:10 PM. Too early for bed, too dark to read. He remembered the emergency candles in his kitchen drawer, a gift from his mother when he'd moved in six months ago. "You never know," she'd said, and he'd rolled his eyes. Now, as he lit the first one, the small flame casting shadows that danced across his walls. He felt a flicker of gratitude.

The building settled into the kind of quiet that only comes with a power outage. No TV sounds bleeding through walls, no washing machines spinning, no elevator hum. Just the rain against his window. Looking around the now dimly lit room, Ryo retrieved his food from the counter. *At least I have this*, he thought. He began to eat but something made him pause.

Footsteps.

Ryo tilted his head, listening. They were coming from the corridor outside, moving with a strange regularity. Not the hurried steps of someone searching for a flashlight or checking on neighbors, but steady and rhythmic.

More footsteps joined the first, falling into the same mono-tonic rhythm. Curious, Ryo moved to his door and peered through the peephole. In the darkness of the hallway, he could make out the glow of a phone light moving past. Yamamoto-san from 6C, he recognized her floral house dress. She walked stiffly, her free arm swaying in time with her steps.

Behind her, another light appeared. And another. His neigh-bors, walking in procession, all matching with that steady pace.

Ryo opened his door slightly, holding his candle. The small flame revealed Suzuki-san from 6A, the young salary man who usually rushed past with a quick bow. Now he moved with the same mechanical gait as Yamamoto-san, his face slack and eyes fixed ahead.

They were all walking toward the end of the corridor. Toward Unit 6E.

Ryo frowned. Nobody lived in 6E. The previous tenant had moved out weeks before he had arrived, and the building manager had mentioned something about repairs being needed before it could be rented again. He'd never seen the door opened, never heard sounds from within.

Yet now, in the darkness, his neighbors moved toward it like iron filings drawn to a magnet. Even the old man from 6D, who rarely left his apartment, shuffled past Ryo's door in his house slippers, his footsteps punctuated only by the tap of his walking stick as he moved.

Lightning flashed again, and in that instant, Ryo saw what his candle's glow had not been strong enough to reveal – all of his neighbors were smiling. Not their usual polite smiles of passing recognition, but wide, empty grins that didn't reach their eyes.

Thunder cracked all around and Ryo jumped, nearly dropping his candle. The flame flickered, sending shadows skittering across the walls. He counted his neighbors as they passed: seven, eight, nine. Everyone from the sixth floor.

A sound drifted back from the direction of Unit 6E – a low hum, which Ryo felt through the soles of his slippers rather than heard. It matched the rhythm of their footsteps perfectly. Ryo's heartbeat quickened as he realized he could feel it in his chest too, like a beat from a distant drum.

He should close his door. Call the police, maybe. With his free hand, he pulled his phone from his pocket. No signal. *The storm must've knocked out the mast*, he thought. Replacing the phone back in his pocket, he knew he should close the door but something made his hesitate. The rhythm of the footsteps had stopped, replaced only by silence.

His neighbors had stopped moving. They stood uniformly around Unit 6E's door, still swaying slightly. Their mix of phone and candle lights created overlapping pools of brightness on the floor of different hues and intensities but all pulsing in unison now. Even their breathing seemed synchronized.

Ryo pressed himself against the wall, trying to stay in the shadows. The faint humming he had heard before was getting louder, as if it were traveling right through him. The light seeping from beneath the door of Unit 6E wasn't steady, like someone's emergency lighting. It pulsed. Brightened and dimmed. Brightened and dimmed.

Like a heartbeat.

His own heart lurched, trying to match the rhythm. His body wanted to sway with the others. The candle trembled in his hand, its flame dancing to the same awful tempo.

The door to Unit 6E began to open.

Ryo wanted to run, but his feet felt heavy, anchored to the floor. The humming was all around him now, pressing against his eardrums. His neighbors' faces turned toward the widening gap, their empty smiles growing broader.

Light spilled out not the warm glow of candles, but something colder. Bluer. More alive. It pulsed with purpose, each beat sending waves of shadow down the corridor, but there was something about it that felt profoundly wrong. Something false, like a broken promise.

A sharp pain in his hand broke the spell. The candle had burned down, hot wax spilling over his fingers. He hissed and dropped it, the flame extinguishing instantly. In that moment of pain, the humming weakened its hold just enough. Ryo stumbled backward, fighting the urge to look through the door of Unit 6E.

As one, his neighbors stepped toward, moving into the pulsing light. Yamamoto-san first, then Suzuki-san, then the others. Their shadows stretched behind them, growing longer and darker with each pulse of light, until they seemed to blend together into a single mass of shifting darkness.

No, Ryo thought. He closed his eyes tightly, focusing on the burn on his hand. Anything to resist the drumbeat pulling him inside. He wouldn't let it drag him in. With gritted teeth, he clutched his hand, fighting against the force. Gradually, the pulse began fade, until only silence and darkness remained.

Ryo slumped to the ground, not daring to open his eyes. The seconds ticked by, counted only by his ragged breaths. Through his closed eyes, Ryo saw the lights flicker back on, flooding the hallway with harsh, artificial brightness.

As the hum of the building settled back to normal, Ryo slowly opened his eyes, blinking in the harsh light. The corridor was empty, doors shut tight, the silence deep and thick. He staggered to his feet, catching his reflection in a window – eyes wide, face pale, like a stranger looking back at him. For a moment, he thought he could still feel the faint echo of that pulse beneath his skin, as if a part of it lingered, buried but not gone.

Around him was only silence. The door of Unit 6E was closed.

# 13

# Silicon Princess

*Author's Note*

*I first came across the Japanese tale of Princess Kaguya while visiting the Young V&A museum in London with my eldest son. It was the summer break, and we'd seen that they were hosting a temporary exhibition called Japan: Myths to Manga. My son and I are both big Manga fans, so we got up early and took the train into London. The exhibition was wonderful, as was the museum itself. We learned so much about traditional Japanese mythology and folklore and had great fun with all the interactive elements of the show. Dotted around the walls at regular intervals were plaques outlining different Japanese myths which inspired classic Anime and Manga, one of which was 'The Tale of Princess Kaguya'.*

*The tale often cited as one of the oldest examples of science fiction. It tells the story of a mysterious princess discovered as a tiny, radiant being inside a bamboo stalk by a bamboo cutter and his wife. As she grows into a stunningly beautiful woman, noblemen and even the emperor seek her hand in marriage, but she sets them impossible tasks to win her favor. Eventually, it is revealed that she is from the*

*Moon, and despite her parents' love, she must return to her celestial home, leaving the world in sorrow. I wanted to re-imagine this tale in the modern world but from the perspective of one of her suitors and how obsession and desperation would drive them even in the face of an impossible task.*

I first saw her in person at the tech conference in a crisp white suit, her jet-black hair a stark contrast to the paleness of her skin. She moved across the stage like water, keeping everyone transfixed with her hypnotic voice as she unveiled her company's new products. Each one more breathtaking than the last.

I've since seen that face many times online. She rebuilt that company on her own in just two years. It had floundered for years under the leadership of her adopted father, never fulfilling its potential. After his health started to fail, she took up the role of CEO, and quickly turned things around, picking up funding and investment as she went. Unlike many of the companies in Silicon Valley, hers actually made good on their promises, justifying those investments with quick product releases and fast returns. Her face, shining like moonlight, always accompanying all corporate communication.

Like many, I was drawn to her. I had to learn her secrets. After seeing her in person, I followed all her channels, desperate to pick up anything I could apply to my own career or my life in general. It was there she issued her challenge. Five impossible tasks for five eager apprentices. The prize? Her mind, her future. An equal partnership in the company she'd built. I was chosen along with four others. My task? To create the ultimate unbreakable encryption.

"*If you can devise an encryption I cannot break in 24 hours, the prize will be yours.*"

Her voice was melodious, her face reminding me of the stars themselves. It still haunts my dreams.

For months, I've done nothing but work on this encryption. My apartment is a cave of discarded energy drink cans and takeout containers. Whiteboards cover every wall, scrawled with algorithms and mathematical proofs. My computer hums constantly, running simulations and tests. Everything I send to her gets sent back; my latest attempt, along with my hopes, broken in hours.

I see her everywhere. On every whiteboard, in every blink of the cursor. Sometimes, I even swear she's in the room with me. I catch subtle hints of cherry blossom in the air; the moonlight at night moves shadows around me like the dancing of her hair as she walks.

But the code eludes me. I've tried everything. Quantum key distribution, homomorphic encryption, even esoteric mathematical concepts that most cryptographers dismiss as fantasies. Nothing is good enough. Nothing is worthy of her. It all gets sent back.

The others have all given up on their tasks already. The AI ethicist couldn't create a truly empathetic artificial intelligence. The geneticist couldn't splice aging out of human DNA. The physicist couldn't create a stable lab-based wormhole. The neuroscientist couldn't map every neural connection in the brain.

I'm the last one standing, but my time is running out.

Sometimes, in my more lucid moments, I wonder if this is what she wanted all along. Not a suitor, not a partner, but a catalyst. Helping her push the boundaries of science in our desperation to win her approval.

But then I remember the way her eyes softened when she looked at me, the tremor in her voice when she explained my task. There was longing there, wasn't there? A hope that one of us would succeed where all others had failed.

Or perhaps I'm just projecting.

The truth is that it doesn't matter. I'm in too deep now. My world has narrowed to this single point of focus – the perfect, unbreakable code. My impossible task. My key to Kaguya's heart.

I turn back to my computer, fingers poised over the keyboard. One more try. One more algorithm. One more chance to prove myself worthy of a woman who fell from the stars.

The cursor blinks. I begin again.

# 14

# The Falls

*Author's Note*

*I wanted to finish this collection with a monster tale. I came across the Japanese myth of the Jorogumo while researching folklore from around the world. For those who haven't heard of this story before, the Jorogumo is often depicted as a shape-shifting spider spirit (Yokai) that can transform into a beautiful woman to ensnare her victims. There are a few famous legends of the Jorogumo. One of the most well-known is the woodcutter tale set near the Jōren Waterfall, where a young man is drawn to a mysterious woman. After a warning from a monk, he discovers her true nature as a spider spirit, leading to his escape. I wanted to imagine a tale where the Jorogumo was still out there, waiting for another victim. Sorry Haruki...*

*Warnings: Adult Themes, Violence*

"I'm so lost" Haruki thought. Despite his heritage, this was the first time he'd visited Japan. Having spent most of his life in the south of England, it was all a bit of a culture shock. He didn't really know why he was out here. Time and decisions had all gone by in a blur these last few months. Growing up, his father had always wanted him to take more time to explore his past, telling Haruki stories of his own youth back in Japan, making sure Haruki knew of his heritage. However, Haruki had always considered himself more English, seeing more of himself in his mother's lineage than his father's. He knew it quietly upset his father that he didn't pay more attention to his stories but connecting with others, even his own family, had always been difficult. Now his father was gone, Haruki felt it was time to finally work on this side of himself. The loneliness had felt too oppressive for too long. He longed for more human connection.

He'd arrived in Tokyo the previous week with only a rough outline of a plan, and had spent the first few days trying to acclimatize. He knew a little of the language and was glad he at least paid attention to some of his father's teachings, but not enough to feel integrated. Even though he felt very much between worlds, he was determined to make the most of his time. It was connection that he was here for, to his past and to his future. He didn't have many expectations of the trip, but he did promise himself he'd visit his father's hometown of Izu, a coastal city a few hours' drive west of Tokyo in the Shizuoka prefecture. His father had told him lots about this city, about its lush forests, hot springs and the famous Jōren Falls. He was keen to experience it for himself. It was where his mother and father had met. His mother had always found it so easy to make friends, something Haruki envied, and she'd given him a lot of useful advice about the trip. She was always gently encouraging Haruki to be more adventurous, to leave his comfort zone from time-to-time. Now he was here, it was up to him.

Arriving in the city, he had a plan to visit the Falls first and then, leaving his car, hike some local trails. Having spent a lot of his free time exploring the southern downs in England when he was younger, he was confident following trails and reading maps. The outdoors, he understood; it was people he always found difficult. Spending time with others left him drained and he often used the solitude of walking to recharge at weekends.

During his time at university, Haruki had envied those who spent their time outside class partying, but it was never something that came easily to him. After a while he'd just stopped trying. University wasn't quite the experience he'd been hoping for, and he'd left feeling more alone and more disconnected from the world than when he'd started.

It was the height of tourist season, and the sun was shining when he arrived at Jōren Waterfalls. A large storm was forecast for later, so he guessed people had come out early to make the best of the good weather. He saw a lot of local and international visitors but didn't feel a part of either group. It was remarkable how lonely it felt even among so many people. The Falls were pleasant although not spectacular. He took a short tour around a wasabi farm located nearby but the rest of the tour group were families or older couples. Feeling dejected, Haruki left as soon as he could. The experience left him drained and he needed to recharge. The solitude of the trails was calling and craving some time to himself, he headed out.

~

*This was a bad idea*, Haruki thought after following yet another small path that came to nothing. He'd long since lost track of the web of paths he'd followed and was now deep in the forest. When he'd started out, the main trail was busy with other people, especially as he moved away from Jōren Falls, but the further he went, the fewer people he saw. The trail was wide, well signposted and clearly well maintained. When he came to the turnaround point he saw a small, single-track path leading away from the main trail. Nothing was visible beyond but dense forest, but he had a map, some water and snacks and, bored of the cultivated path he'd been walking on so far, he decided to explore it.

It was getting later now however, and Haruki began to panic; a couple of hours into his detour, his food was gone, and he knew the light would begin to fade soon. More worryingly though, no one knew he was out here. Around him, in the watery evening light, he could see the glistening of large webs, dotted by small yellow and black spiders, their long, silken strands tight like biwa strings. He was constantly brushing them away from himself, though they were invisible to him as he walked. He stopped and forced himself to stay calm. Remembering his old map reading skills, he knew to look for way points but there was nothing in this dense forest he could use as landmarks. The forest felt uncomfortably close and there was silence all around him. He had been so used to the sound of the river that he hadn't noticed until then that the sound of the running water had stopped. How far had he gone exactly?

"You look lost."

A smooth, confident sounding voice suddenly cut through the silence behind him. Haruki whirled around. He hadn't heard anyone approach. Standing in front of him, about ten paces away, was a girl. She had an oval face and looked hardly older than twenty. She was barefoot and was looking at him intensely, though her lips bore a faint smile. Her eyes were large and dark but with a small hint of bright yellow in the centers. Haruki stared back, brushing more webs from his face.

"Yeah, I came off the main trail and can't remember my way back," He said, forcing some composure into his features.

"Come with me, I'll take you back," she and stepped toward him, taking his hand.

The suddenness of physical contact was like electricity up Haruki's arm, spreading in an instant throughout his body. Her hand, though small, encased his tightly, binding them together. He stood there, unsure of what to say or do; he was completely out of his element.

"What is your name?" she asked, as they began to walk. She was so close to him that despite the cool evening, Haruki could feel her body heat.

"Haruki," he said tentatively, remembering to breathe.

"Haruki," she repeated, as if playing with the sound of it. "It's nice to meet you, Haruki."

"What's yours?" Haruki asked, trying to keep his voice as steady as he could. He noticed then, for the first time, that they were speaking in English.

She leaned in close to him. "My name?" she inquired, looking slightly amused. After a few moments, she replied: "You can call me Emiko."

Haruki felt the words rather than hearing them, as if he'd somehow already known. She smiled and held his gaze for a few seconds longer, still holding his hand as they continued on. Haruki had so many more questions but couldn't bring himself to speak. Her hand felt so good around his own. She felt part of him.

After a short while, they arrived back at the main trail, the clear signpost pointing the way back to Jōren Falls.

"You're going back to the Falls?" she asked. Haruki nodded awkwardly, unable to drag his eyes away from hers. "I'll walk with you" she told him. It wasn't a request, and he wasn't about to refuse anyway.

"Were you hiking out here?" Haruki finally managed to ask as they began walking back toward the Falls.

The last of the evening light was fading now, and he noticed how cold it was getting. Dark clouds were gathering above and the air felt heavy. *The storm must be getting close*, he thought. It didn't seem to bother Emiko, however. She had no warm clothes, wearing a simple white top and black shorts, but she seemed quite comfortable despite the cool air.

"Are you cold?" Haruki asked, starting to remove his jacket to offer her. He'd been walking in a daze, and he was only now remembering how light her clothing was. How had she got all the way out here like this?

"I love walking in the evening. It's OK, you can keep that," she said with an amused smile as he held out the jacket. "I always come out here," she continued. "I don't always meet lost young men like you though." Her smile widened. She held his hand tighter for a moment and moved slightly closer, so they were walking shoulder to shoulder. Haruki's body tightened.

"Do you live in Izu? You're English is very good." Haruki had no idea what to say but he wanted to keep this connection. He'd never been this close to someone before, and he didn't want to lose it.

"I live close to the Falls. Lots of people visit here from all over the world. It's remarkable what you can pick up from listening to people."

Now they were speaking, Haruki wanted to make sure the conversation continued. "My father grew up in Izu," he offered, "and I've never visited here before. He used to tell me lots of stories about his time here as a child and I wanted to see it for myself. He passed away recently."

Emiko turned to him abruptly. "What stories did he tell you about Jōren Falls?"

Feeling panicked at Emiko's sudden change of tone, Haruki offered a quick reply. "He told me about how he used to come to the rivers with my grandfather to fish and how he'd play in the forest with his brother and sister looking for Joro spiders. He and my mother first met here. She came here when she was traveling around Asia and wanted to improve her Japanese, so he used to help her." Emiko looked straight ahead as he spoke, and Haruki was suddenly worried he'd ruined it. "He always wanted me to come here," he continued, trying to salvage things. "But I don't know how to fish, and I'm scared of spiders!" He offered her a tentative laugh.

Emiko smiled contentedly, then abruptly stopped and turned to Haruki again, her dark, wide eyes reaching into his. In one fluid movement, she raised up on her tiptoes and softly kissed him on the cheek.

"You don't need to be scared of spiders," she whispered in his ear.

Haruki stood frozen. Emiko was shorter than him by a head, but it was like she was all around him, sharing his entire existence, tightening their connection. He again felt the warmth radiating from her body as she lightly touched his chest.

"Come with me," she breathed.

The dying ends of evening were now making way for night but there was enough light from the moon still visible among the darkening clouds for them to see their way. Emiko moved lightly and confidently, her bare feet brushing over the ground.

By contrast, Haruki felt awkward and ungainly in his heavy hiking boots. A small path moved away from the main trail which Emiko guided them toward. After that kiss, he would have followed her anywhere. Haruki could hear the Falls in the distance, all the daytime visitors now gone. It was just the two of them now.

From the darkness along the path, they emerged into a clearing in the forest. A wooden cabin stood in the center. It was small and looked like it had been skillfully constructed from the forest itself. Stacked logs formed all four walls with a sturdy, sloping roof covered in vegetation. Trees from all around them had been felled here to make room for it and there were still many stumps with axe marks at their bases. Small wooden carvings hung off the lowest branches of the remaining trees and as they approached the house, Haruki observed how intricate they were, the detail still visible in the semi-darkness.

"Did you make these?" he asked.

"Not me," Emiko responded. "Someone who I used to be close to." She let go of his hand to open the door. It swung inwards and she backed through the threshold, holding his gaze with those large eyes. Haruki followed, all other thoughts leaving his mind.

After removing his heavy shoes at the door, Haruki noticed how warm it was inside although there was no sign of a fire, and no power could've reached this far into the forest. The house was one large room lit only with dozens of candles. The sounds of the waterfall outside were no longer audible. It was like entering another world. Shadows from the candlelight flickered and crawled, yellow and black across everything in Haruki's vision as he took in the room around him.

Emiko moved silently toward a large traditional futon in the center of the room, beckoning Haruki to follow. Her dark, yellow-flecked eyes seeming to intensify in the candlelight.

As they sat together on the futon, Emiko leaned close, her breath warm against his ear. "You don't need to be afraid," she whispered again. "I'll take care of you."

She kissed him, a soft, lingering kiss that sent waves of heat coursing through his body. It was unlike anything he had ever experienced before, and he found himself surrendering to it completely. Emiko's hands moved with practiced skill, removing his jacket and shirt, then lingering teasingly at the fastenings of his trousers. Haruki was powerless under her touch, his world narrowing to the points where their bodies connected.

With gentle guidance, Emiko placed Haruki's hands at the hem of her top. He lifted it slowly, revealing smooth, pale skin that seemed to glow in the candlelight. As she pressed herself against him, his senses were overwhelmed – the taste of her lips, the softness of her skin, the scent that was uniquely hers.

Emiko's movements were slow and deliberate at first, building a rhythm that matched the flickering of the candles around them. Haruki watched as the shadows danced across her body as she moved, flickering and crawling, yellow and black across everything in his vision. Outside, the storm that had been threatening all evening finally broke. Thunder crashed around the cabin, and the sound of rain on the roof was like thousands of tiny footsteps scurrying across the world.

Lost in the moment, Haruki surrendered himself completely to the experience. This connection, this intimacy, was something he had never thought possible. He would have given anything for it to last forever.

Emiko's pace increased, her grip on him tightening as she

took control. She pushed him down onto his back, pinning his wrists above his head as she moved with greater intensity. The candles seemed to flare brighter, their light pulsing in time with their shared rhythm.

A bolt of lightning illuminated the room, bright as day for a split second. In that flash, Haruki caught a glimpse of Emiko's face transformed. Her eyes were wide, solid black with bursts of bright yellow, and her teeth were bared in a feral grin. The sight sent a jolt of fear through him.

Emiko's grip tightened further, her movements growing more frenzied. Haruki felt something tighten around his wrists and ankles – invisible threads binding him in place. Panic began to rise in his chest, warring with the waves of pleasure still coursing through his body.

*What is she doing?* The thought flashed through Haruki's mind as he struggled against his bonds. He tried to cry out, to tell her to stop, but found his voice silenced, his mouth bound shut.

Emiko moved faster still, her eyes wild. As the sensations peaked, Emiko's nails scratched deep into his chest as she suddenly lunged toward, sharp teeth piercing the soft flesh of Haruki's neck.

Pain exploded through him as his blood gushed, hot and sticky. Emiko held him tight, her teeth buried deep in his flesh. The edges of Haruki's vision began to darken, the room around him transforming. A cold wind cut through the warm air, chilling the mix of blood and sweat that covered his body. Emiko's form, pressed tightly against him, now felt like ice.

As consciousness began to slip away, Haruki became aware of thousands of tiny movements all around him. In the fading candlelight, he caught flashes of yellow and black crawling over his body, their needle-like pincers piercing his skin.

As they overwhelmed him, Emiko released him and sat back. That faint smile still showed across her face, now glistening with blood in the candlelight. The bright yellow of her eyes pierced through the darkness. As the room and everything else faded from Haruki's consciousness, he heard Emiko's voice one last time.

"Thank you, Haruki. I meant what I said. I will take care of you now."

His eyes, like the webs all around him, closed.

# About the Author

Hi, I'm Alex. I was born in London but but now live in the historic town of Amesbury, England, a place rich with ancient history and folklore. Living near Stonehenge, with its air of mystery, is fueling my imagination, inspiring much of the mythological and legendary elements in my writing. The power of old stories—of gods, monsters, and heroes—speaks to me, and I strive to reflect that in the worlds I create.

I'm a husband, a father to two young boys, and the owner of a bouncy labradoodle named Sonic. These roles offer me a perspective that shapes the themes I return to time and again—of love, loss, and the fragility of time itself. In the quiet moments between family life, I find the inspiration to create.

**You can connect with me on:**

🌐 https://www.darkfellwrites.com

🖇 https://www.instagram.com/alex_darkfellwrites

**Subscribe to my newsletter:**

✉ https://www.darkfellwrites.com